A Bullet in His Forehead

A Bullet in
His Forehead

Manuel Aguirre

Translated from the Spanish by
Santiago Aguirre

DEDICATION

To my father José Aurelio who, after intense suffering, died in perfect peace on the 17th of February 2004

"Lord, let my forks and medals rust,
My molars rot;
Drive my barber insane;
May my servants be killed in their wooden beds,
But deliver me from the devil."

ANTONIO CISNEROS

ACKNOWLEDGMENTS

Special thanks to my dear friend, Bill Staton, for his wonderful, tireless, and unselfish proof-reading of this translation.

CONTENTS

1	Eleuterio	15
2	Stubby Ligurio	31
3	At the Break of Dawn	36
4	Eleodoro & Virginia	45
5	Destiny's Overseer	62
6	The Guy Was a Queer	75
7	Delirium	85
8	The Ghost	106
9	Rules of the Game	114
10	And What If There Were No God?	122
11	Leoncio and His 'Pops'	138
12	Virgilio's Freedom	149
13	Before a White Brick Wall	158
	About the Author	171
	The Saga	172

ELEUTERIO

The administrator of the Ninantaya Hacienda, a second lieutenant in the Peruvian Army, opens his eyes in the dark and senses that his entire body is in a state of absolute wakefulness. Finding himself immersed in this strange predicament, a jolt of terror shakes him to the core. Trapped in a labyrinth of fear, the young military man breathes a worried sigh for he is more than aware of the danger that lies buried in the actions he has planned for tomorrow at dawn.

The inexperienced cavalry officer, Gerardo Arrieta, has been informed by the inhabitants of the hacienda under his supervision, that the Bolivians, on the other side of the border, usually travel armed; that they have itchy trigger fingers and tend to shoot at anything that moves from anywhere they can hide behind without thinking about the consequences. Most of them have simply grown up killing one another to maintain this confrontational tradition. "It has always been this way around these parts and nothing has ever happened to us yet," they usually say after committing some atrocity. Being aware of this peculiar custom, the young officer fights with his pillow, unable to find any sleep. "It's not that I'm afraid that someone will take my life," he thinks; "what really chills me to the marrow is the thought that one of my men may be killed and that because of this single 'act of fate,' I might be court-martialed and possibly condemned to be a captain for the rest of my life."

* * *

The Ninantaya Hacienda is a fifteen-hundred-acre rectangle of cold, desolate wasteland. One of its shorter sides hugs the territory of neighboring Bolivia. The border in this area of the country, like all other international borders, is hypothetical; it is a simple line drawn by politicians in a complex and whimsical way over ridgelines and ravines that crisscross with the hidden intention of remaining undiscovered.

The majordomo of this large property is Eleuterio. His name was an accident given that his parents, Aimara Indians from the region, never learned Castilian Spanish and knew much less about the Greeks. Eleuterio is a stocky man, short in stature, with an angled face like that of most of the people of the Peruvian Altiplano. When someone asks him his age, he answers with a grin and a mixture of whines and guffaws: "I ain't got no idea, *papitooo*..." The Aimaras tend to prolong the vowel sounds at the end of their words to satisfy an innate cultural need to seem more humble and meek than they really are. The truth is that they think they can gain the upper hand if their interlocutors take pity on them. "Could it be that I'm 'bout forty-fiiive?" asks Eleuterio with a squeaky, child-like voice to anyone who happens to inquire about his age.

However, the Indian's question is an honest one because, just like the rest of his people, he does not have the slightest idea when he was born. The Indians of the Altiplano do not understand the concept of linear time; for them, there are only four seasons occurring one after the other for eternity.

Eleuterio is the only Indian who speaks Castilian Spanish in the Ninantaya Hacienda. This singular ability makes his existence so important that the jocular steward believes himself to be somewhat god-like. Ever since the cavalry officer came to this four-house town, Eleuterio

16

began chiming: "You're the one who's going to retake the little ravine that those damn *Boliches*[1] stole from us in fifty-six, *papitooo!*" In the weeks following the arrival of the young officer, our hacienda's caretaker worked on his new boss with the tenacity of a mule trainer: gradually and persistently, but taking care not to irritate the animal too much. When mules get pass that stage, they generally acquire a stubbornness that not only can never be cured, but also makes them incapable of daily work for the rest of their lives.

* * *

During his six-month stay in the forward operating base at Ninantaya, the second lieutenant dedicated himself to completing near impossible tasks. "I wonder if there is any meaningful work that I can perform in the short amount of time that remains in my detail here?" he asked himself. He speculated that within this brief amount of time his relieving officer would arrive from one of the other military bases in the region and, upon completing his six months, he too would be replaced by another and this last one by yet another; as such, without conspiring to do so, all these officer-administrators will end up bringing ever-increasing disorder and misery to this small corner of reality. Nevertheless, consistent with his obsession for planning, he put himself to work and gave free reign to his imagination. He wanted to build a mud-brick watchtower so tall that it would allow him to keep an eye on the bordering country to the south, just one league from his house. At the same time, he sought to patrol, twenty-four-hours a day, the twenty-two and a half mile border assigned to him by his superiors, using the ten soldiers under his command. It was for this reason that Eleuterio began to worry about the second

---

[1] Peruvians use this derogatory term to refer to Bolivians.

lieutenant's mental state. However, the majordomo could only interpret these feelings when he was by himself in the plains. On these occasions, he would bow his head and sway it from side to side while drilling his temple with his hand in the shape of a gun. Afterwards, Eleuterio would mutter: "All of them come and go but, when it comes down to it, I am the only one that remains and runs this town." Then, walking proudly, he returned to his daily chores.

Twenty-four families of *colonos*[2] make up the Ninantaya Hacienda and they live right in the middle of the pampa on the western side of that property which happens to belong to the Peruvian Army. Their houses, as is typical in these kinds of communities, are spaced some six hundred feet apart from each other. The lives of these people are very quiet, solitary, and so independent, that the second lieutenant concluded that each family comprised its own country. Their leader was Eleuterio, the majordomo of the hacienda that the Spaniards first created and then superimposed over the rectangular shaped piece of land that had always been those Aimaras' natural home.

A little while before the second lieutenant took charge of the hacienda Eleuterio got married. His wife's name was Adoración and she was about twenty-two years old when her parents gave her away so that she could set up her own home. Eleuterio loves her with all his heart. When he finds himself alone in the pampas, on the lookout for any passers-by that may cross the border, he speaks aloud to himself. "Well," he says, "I am not alone, *taititaaa*; I am with

---

[2] This term derives from the Latin *colonus*, which land owners used in Europe during the early feudal period to refer to those laborers that those same landowners eventually called serfs. The Spaniards in the Americas would later use this designation as of the 16th century (and the Peruvians until the present day) to refer to the indigenous population working as serfs on their haciendas in the Altiplano region.

myseeelf," he explains, with a loud guffaw and shooting his characteristic smile that beamed with satisfaction, the satisfaction of being him.

"I can speak with anyone," asserts Eleuterio. During these moments, the Indian preaches to the wind of his love for Adoración, his young wife. He speaks with the plants, caresses their leaves, and cleans them with his fat fingers that are rough as sandpaper. To them he explains the innumerable tasks he must complete so that they may live, bear fruit, and exhibit these immediately to everyone to justify their existence. When the wind picks up, Eleuterio turns his body and spins on his toes. The majordomo howls to the heavens with joy in the middle of the whirlwind that envelops him, and affirms that Adoración means everything to him. He proclaims that his heart flutters when he is in her presence, just like the little wings on those butterflies that, as they say, flit about the flowers over there in Cuzco, where it is not as cold as it is here.

When he thinks about her, his chest fills up with something that he cannot describe because he has never felt this way before. "It's like a marvelous liquid, like a drunkenness that I feel under my ribs and fills my whole body in such a way that it makes me want to cry. But, I don't let any tears come to my eyes because I am the most important man in this place. So, I leave the house and come back only at night, when I am calm and collected and she is asleep and no longer able to look at me."

Eleuterio has never spoken to his wife. "She is such a little *thiiing*. So much younger than me and, well, I'm so dignified. But I love her very *muuuch*. That's for sure." Some days ago, Eleuterio insisted on talking about his future. He says he is going to have many children with Adoración; that they will be three boys to help him herd their sheep and two girls to weave ponchos and *awayus*[3].

---

[3] A colorful shawl made of sheep or alpaca wool, used by Aimara women to transport their babies on their backs.

"Adoración is going to provide me with a little one very soon, that's for sure", he says between laughs, brimming with happiness; yet Eleuterio is unaware that his beloved does not sleep well. Night after night, she suffers from nefarious nightmares that do not allow her to get any rest at all. Every morning, Adoración grapples with the bitter memory of her bad dream, but after considerable effort, overcomes the anguish, forgetting the threat of death that in her dreams weighs heavily against her husband.

* * *

Soon enough, the second lieutenant, under the daily pressure of Eleuterio's goading, began to ruminate over the project that the caretaker had been imploring him to consider. The hacienda's commanding officer made calculations on a large sheet of paper that he had spread out over his dining room table. "He draws hills and lines, little circles and crosses. He measures with his ruler and jots down a whole bunch of numbers that even I don't know about *yeeet*", Eleuterio would say to the wind, every evening on his walk back to his plot of land.

According to Eleuterio, the second lieutenant justified the plan's delay by claiming that it is difficult to acquire a steel drum like those that truckers travelling throughout the region utilize to transport gasoline; he argued that the task is as difficult as finding a nuclear submarine in Lake Titicaca. The officer added, "In this shitty town, if one can even call it a town, there are only four houses: the police station, the post office, the school, and the customs house." But finally, the second lieutenant managed to confiscate a rusty steel drum from a Bolivian truck. In this receptacle, which was the only one of its kind in that area, the military officer explained that it would be possible for them to pour down concrete, and thus create a replica of the border marker that the Bolivians stole back in fifty-six.

* * *

Adoración doesn't have anyone to talk to because she's not from the town of Ninantaya. Eleuterio got her from Rucano, a city far to the north from where they live. But even still, she is very happy. She worships her husband. She often thinks that true happiness, as her mother always told her, comes from contemplating her husband's face as he puts into his mouth the food that she meticulously prepared for him. That her felicity as a wife, stems from sensing the joy reflected in Eleuterio's eyes and the excitement in his mouth, as he chews the boiled potatoes from the quinoa soup that she spent an entire day cooking, amidst sighs of love.

Adoración never speaks to her husband. She simply cannot. She believes herself to be too young for him. She knows, as well, that her husband is a very important man because he's the only one that can speak Castilian Spanish. Thirdly, Eleuterio travels to Bolivia, to a very big city called La Paz, and lastly, her husband must handle the second lieutenant who happens to be the "master" of the land where they built their home. Thus, Adoración is elated when she thinks about Eleuterio sitting on the floor, covered with his poncho. She imagines him eating a stew that she prepared as he warms his feet near the fire in the middle of the room, where they will later lay down to sleep. The woman stares into the eyes of her man and sees how happiness springs forth from them in white, purple, and yellow sparks. Adoración observes his smiling cheeks, taut and smooth, and thinks that there is no other way he can better exhibit his great joy.

21

After she's done eating, she lies down and awaits Eleuterio who, with great care, delicately takes her and possesses her as if she were a crystal figurine. With closed eyes and in absolute silence, Adoración relishes this moment, is happy and begins to fall asleep in the arms of the man who allows her to enjoy life in all its fullness. Afterwards, in search of pleasant dreams she lulls herself with thoughts of the children that will soon be arriving.

However, since nothing is perfect in this world, for seven days now, Adoración has been suffering a horrible nightmare. In it, a rachitic dog with bristly hair, and eyes as yellow as the sun, barks in her ear at an unbearably loud volume, repeating to the point of exhaustion that he is going to eat Eleuterio. "All of him!" he growls with a hollow, putrid, and sarcastic voice, "even the hairs on his head!"

When the long-awaited day arrives, Eleuterio begins to believe fervently that his destiny will play out in much the same way that he has been predicting to the wind for the last few days. Once his boss reinstalls that border marker number twelve, which the locals say the Bolivians stole in nineteen fifty-six, the international border is going to shift, twenty-four- hundred feet inside of what is currently Bolivia, and consequently Eleuterio's famous ravine will once more be within the confines of the Ninantaya Hacienda. This *quebradita*, as the majordomo calls it, is a small valley whose slopes dip forty-five degrees on each side. Thanks to these gradients and the tendency of the ravine to zigzag at that point, it's possible for the locals to cultivate in the *quebradita*, oca and ulluco, two tubers that are not native to these desolate, high plains. "One can even grow lettuce in some good years, *papitooo*," Eleuterio would often repeat, grossly exaggerating the ravine's selling points.

* * *

The members of the group, under the second lieutenant's command, march in a single column. The soldiers advance in silence, carrying the empty steel drum, their allotted weapons, and a machine gun that they never used to take with them in the past, "because it was too much gun for minor situations," as the cavalry officer was prone to say. It was different this time; the soldiers can tell. They ask, "Why the machine gun, Corporal Sulla?" or "This M52 weighs too damn much, Sergeant Mayu! Why do we have to carry it now, if we've never used it before?"

They sent both the sacks of cement and the sand bags the day before in a truck. The second lieutenant had punished a Bolivian driver with this mission for having broken the barrier gate on the road, in front of his command post in Ninantaya. The officer took the opportunity and rendered his judgment, as if he were still in the military academy: "For breaking the gate, damn it, you're going to carry these fucking sacks of sand and cement right up to the international fucking border. You will leave them there, on the side of the road, and then you may return to your goddamn routine. This is your punishment!" He said to the driver, who went away, bowing to the officer, and saying innumerable times "thank you, thank you very much, *jefecitooo*." All the while, however, he kept scratching his head, dumbfounded by the order to bring sand and cement to a freezing desert without any houses or people.

* * *

On top of the hillock, next to the small crater left by the famous missing border marker, the soldiers on watch, shivering with cold, are ready to fire the machinegun. They have been standing inside a narrow trench all day and have been unable to exercise their legs ever since they came to that mound overlooking the ravine. When they had gotten into the foxhole, at dawn, the second lieutenant had encouraged them to shoot off a couple of long bursts, which sounded like an electric sewing machine in high gear. Afterwards, they spent the entire day guarding the perimeter, scanning the hills in search of men on the other side, but they could not see anything out of the ordinary. However, the two privates and the corporal behind the automatic weapon are prisoners of their own fear. They cannot explain why, but they are afraid of something out there. A strange sensation in the pit of their stomachs tells them that something bad is about to happen.

That day, at three o'clock in the afternoon, the men, who were working to fix the mess on the international border, stand up, sweaty and exhausted, on the summit of the hillock. They remember carving out a trench for the machine gun very early this morning, and that afterwards they enlarged the small crater so that they could set up the new border marker. Lastly, they mixed the concrete and poured it into the empty steel drum. They waited some minutes before the concrete started to harden. Then, they polished the convex surface and on it scratched two lines from the center, one pointing towards the next border marker and the other towards the previous one. Now, they look at their hands, dirty and blistery, and spit on them. They rub them together, turn their faces towards their boss, and sigh as if they were waiting for something nobody could possibly predict.

The second lieutenant says, "That's it! We did it! There you go, Eleuterio. There is your damn ravine! Now you won't bust my balls about it every morning with the same old song that, 'you gotta retake the *quebradita* for me,

24

jefecitooo.'" And when he looks for the majordomo, he finds him sitting at the bottom of his *quebradita,* rubbing both the leaves and flowers of sprouting potato plants; speaking to them with tenderness, and, at times, emphasizing his words by raising his index finger as if he were either warning or threatening them, but always with a smile.

* * *

As soon as Eleuterio had seen that the second lieutenant had completed his mission, the majordomo proceeded to meander down the hill towards the plants that the *Boliches* had been growing in his *quebradita* without saying a word to anyone. He had approached a square patch of flowering potato plants and sat down on the ground to be with them.

It was here that the second lieutenant found him caressing the plants and kissing their white, purple, and yellow flowers. The blue sky stretches infinitely in the distance. The sun, weakening by the hour, leans against the ravine's upper edges as it begins to set. Eleuterio raises his hand to gauge the temperature of the environment; he gives approving smiles to the marvelous slopes of those hills, whose forty-five degree angles will allow *his* plants to dodge the effects of ground frost and leave them to grow to maturity.

Eleuterio was brimming over with happiness at the thought of his ravine. He remembers Adoración and promises himself that the following day's task will be to bring her to enjoy this marvel still without a name. "Despite everything," he says in a loud voice, "with the gunfire that the second lieutenant unleashed this morning, no *Boliche* will dare come here, much less shoot at us! They know the sound that my boss' machine gun makes!"

Finished with the task that they started early this morning, the group contemplates, with pride and satisfaction from atop the hillock, the work that had demanded so much of their collective effort. The second lieutenant feeds his ego with images of grandeur and glory in his mind; he pictures the high command congratulating and rewarding him for having returned a sliver of the country that had been in foreign hands because of a cunning usurpation. Meanwhile, the sergeant and the corporal, scratching their cheeks, somberly realize that from here on out they will have to pull guard duty in that trench atop "Eleuterio's ravine" in addition to the many other tasks they already have. Suddenly, Private Huaranga shouts at the man wearing riding boots in a humble, yet ironic, tone of voice, "We've been without food all day, second lieutenant! When are we going to eat, sir?" The young officer understands that this facetious reminder has been a call back to sanity and that without a doubt the soldier is right.

The trek back to their forward operating base in the Ninantaya Hacienda, and a hot meal, will take more than an hour. "Gather up!" shouts the second lieutenant, reassuming full command of the situation, "Take roll sergeant; double check that everyone's accounted for, 'cause we're going back!"

                          *   *   *

He had not even taken ten steps downhill, in the direction of his F.O.B, when they heard the far away sound of a rifle shot. Everyone froze; no one dared move. The second lieutenant, who was staying behind the group because he was adjusting his riding boots, instantly thought to himself, "Rifle shot…small caliber." Next, in less than a second after the rifle report, he heard a buzz in his right ear canal. This was enough to bring him back to reality. Then, the officer reacted. "Sniper! Everyone, get down!" he shouted as he hit the dirt. There, he cogitated with his eyes closed; his mouth filled with soil, dry grass, and a few insects; disgusted, he spat, coughed, and swore several times.

"Everyone on the ground, damn it!" ordered the second lieutenant in a choking voice, "nobody fucking move! I'll kill anyone who stands up!" Feeling a chill down his spine, he thought about the bullet coming from far away, flattened by the journey through the cold air and slowed down by the distance already covered, or by the insufficient amount of powder in the shell. He reflected on the bullet's trajectory with respect to the position of his skull, and gasped when he imagined that it was only four inches to the right of his head. Arrieta could see with his eyes closed, and in a thousand colors, the havoc that that little piece of sharp copper could have wreaked in his brain; in that smooth package of ethereal recollections, ideas, dreams, and realities. Shaking his head nervously like a chained dog, like a savage animal that lost its freedom, he took three deep breaths, pulled himself together and shouted again, "Sergeant Mayu! Are you hit?" After the sergeant answered "negative, sir!" Arrieta went along asking, one by one, how the rest of his men were doing until he came to Eleuterio... but the majordomo didn't answer.

The young officer turned around and saw Eleuterio lying on his back, as if he were sleeping. At first, the second lieutenant believed that the "dumbass Indian" had sprawled on his back when minutes before he shouted, "Everyone on the ground!" After loudly calling his name several times and not getting any response, he felt a cold sensation entering his belly. It traveled down to his testicles and up to the pit of his stomach, trachea, and throat, suffocating him, and producing a kind of pain somewhere between a muffled sob and a sore throat. The second lieutenant stood up, despite the shouts of his men to get back down on the ground to avoid being the target of enemy fire. At that moment, no one knew where the shot came from. The officer walked calmly and without any consideration for his safety. He knelt beside Eleuterio's body and thought of Adoración.

"What would he say to his wife? What, if anything, was he going to say to her...?"

Eleuterio had an entry wound under his right eye. The second lieutenant was certain that a twenty-two caliber bullet caused it because the hole was miniscule, like a fly sitting on the Indian's face. The officer grabbed the majordomo's head by the hair and examined it, inch by inch, in search of the hole through which that little piece of death had made its exit. Behind Eleuterio's left ear, he found a thread of blood that trickled down behind his neck, just under his shirt. The bullet had traversed the fragile bones of his right cheek and circled the interior of his skull without the sufficient amount of force needed to break through the occipital bone, due to the distance the bullet had covered, and ended up exiting through the weakest point: the intricate left inner ear.

For several minutes, the second lieutenant lost control of himself. He shouted, spewed insults, blasphemed, and then, as he became deathly pale, he vomited the few drops of saliva that he had in his stomach. The Indian was dead. "What was he going to say to the majordomo's wife? Why did Eleuterio have to be the victim and not him?" He thought. "Why the fuck, do people die like that; in the blink of an eye; as if they were playing cops and robbers, or as one turns off a radio? Who the hell controls this?" says Arrieta and spits on the ground with fury.

While a cadet, Gerardo Arrieta had learned, by blows, a method for rationalizing situations that appear to be contradictory; that method came to his rescue in this crossroads, renewing a sense of purpose in his life. The second lieutenant's face lit up and he ordered his sergeant to go to the police station in Ninantaya, and bring one of the civil guards to file a report. He would personally escalate the matter to the proper authorities, he said. "This will provoke an international incident, then the Department of State[4] will demand an investigation, and in the end, those responsible for this crime will be punished," he insisted. "But despite all this protocol and all that could be gained by it," thought the second lieutenant, "what will he say to Eleuterio's wife? How was he going to explain to Adoración that they would have to bury Eleuterio?"

When the guardsman Dionisio Maravedí arrived, he walked up to Eleuterio's body. He gently moved him with the tip of his shoe, as if he were searching for the wound, the blood, and said, "I can see nothing wrong with him, Second Lieutenant." The officer answered him in a monotone voice, "He has a fucking hole in his face and he's dead, moron. Why do you think we called you?" The gendarme, with the same initial indifference, answered, "Well, then he is dead; a stray bullet, possibly? It could have been a sniper, Second Lieutenant. There is nothing that we can do, sir. Who can tell me where the shot came from, eh Second Lieutenant? If anything, we need to bury him soon, before he begins to smell." Between shouts and insults, the officer ordered the gendarme to file a report. After a total of forty-five minutes of total miscommunication, Arrieta gave up. He told the civil guard to "go the fuck to hell," and then carried the dead man on the shoulders of his troops.

As he walked back to Ninantaya, after giving it a lot of thought, the officer concluded that the only thing that he could tell Adoración was that a bullet, fired from the hands of a hidden individual on the other side of the border, had killed the majordomo. There was nothing additional that he could do. The Indian woman would have to accept the reality of the situation. Her husband, Eleuterio, was simply dead.

---

[4] In Peru, it's known as the Ministry of Foreign Affairs (or in Spanish, Ministerio de Relaciones Exteriores).

* * *

Eleuterio's burial took three days (with their corresponding nights) of dancing, chewing coca leaves and drinking *cañazo*.[5] The soldiers say that during this time the second lieutenant celebrated with all the Indians, arm-in-arm. And that together they danced forwards and backwards; drank; fell on the floor; and then got up again to keep on dancing. The soldiers stationed at Ninantaya also comment that according to the hacienda's *colonos,* the second lieutenant learned to cry and to speak Aymara during that three-day drinking binge. That while they were dancing with the young officer, the inhabitants of Ninantaya spoke with him about the most intimate details of Eleuterio's life, and that, in the end, after the majordomo's wake, the young officer picked up the damned habit of talking with the wind, every time he walked through the pampa.

* * *

Now, amidst tears, a profound drunkenness brought on by *cañazo,* and the numbness produced by the coca leaves in his mouth, the cavalry officer remembers dancing with that throng of celebrants and reminisces about the tragic event that crisscrosses his mind every evening. It is a nightmare that pushes him against the walls of his room or against the rocks when he sleeps in the hills. It is a bad dream occurring when his eyes are wide open. It is a fatiguing apparition that obliges him to surrender, because he cannot avoid the power of that hallucination.

---

[5] This is a type of 70 proof alcohol made from sugar cane.

30

STUBBY LIGURIO

"The art of war, deafening noises, and physical losses, promiscuously inhabit the same conceptual space," thought Second Lieutenant Arrieta, passing his hand over his pelvis as if palpating for a wound. Upon closing his eyes, he felt a slight chill throughout his body that made him shiver. Seconds later, his face drew forth a crafty smile that instantly burst into a guffaw.

As the overseer of the frontier surveillance post at Ninantaya, in the *Meseta del Collao*, Gerardo Arrieta had the implied task of patrolling twenty-two and a half miles of Peru's border with Bolivia. Given the short amount of time that he had as an army officer (it had only been six months since he was commissioned as second lieutenant) one could say that his life in the highlands surrounding that forward operating base, located to the east of Lake Titicaca, was pure hell. Until recently, he had operated under the machine-like regime of the military academy, a way of life that left its mark on his very soul. As such, he came to believe that it would be possible for him to implement a rigid, "West Point-like" discipline in that *paramo* where, due to certain unimaginable circumstances, he saw himself forced to live.

Despite only having a squad of ten soldiers under his command, Arrieta structured all their activities so that they could conduct patrols twenty-four hours a day. Because of this curious obsession on his part, his soldiers observed him with a bit of apprehension, and thought that, for some strange reason, he was losing his mind. These indigenous conscripts, however, were far from the truth, and because they didn't know what was really troubling their young leader, they mistook this cultural dissonance for insanity.

*   *   *

One day, the second lieutenant found himself touring the dividing line separating Bolivia and Peru, accompanied by one of his soldiers, when a downpour began. Neither of them could see further than ten feet. Contemplating the horrendous rain, Arrieta thought that this phenomenon defied all military logic. He felt like a Lilliputian before this awesome display of nature, and deeply desired to go back in time. He wanted to escape from the world of the military and return to kindergarten; to be a child, and thus slip back under the protective arms of his mother and aunts, to flee from the storm that tormented him in such an inhuman way, "just like when my father used to punish me," he thought. Immediately, he recognized that he was showing weakness and tried to hide it behind a barrage of expletives against the peculiar characteristics of that climate.

In the middle of that torrent, and without shelter, they heard an apocalyptic thunder clap that shook them to the very core. It was an explosion so loud that it ruffled their hair and made their flesh quake as if some giant had grabbed them by the shoulders and jostled them about.

When the second lieutenant heard that ear-piercing boom, his soul trembled, and instantly memories of "Operation Ayacucho," which took place during the middle of his junior year at the military academy, flooded back into his mind. On that occasion, the artillery cadets had screwed up big time. They accidentally changed the coordinates originally aimed at the enemy position. One of the one-hundred-twenty millimeter mortars ended up firing in the direction of the rest of the cadets while they were sleeping, in their foxholes, at the foot of Raven Hill, the place chosen by the generals as their command post. During the prelude to this accident, two of those generals were hotly debating atop this hill (amidst *achupalla* plants, small lizards, and fresh horse excrement) with neither being able to come to an agreement about the length of time needed for the barrage to weaken the enemy position opposite them, on Snail Hill. The severe impasse that caused this dilemma arose from the semantics of a word in the text that guided this hypothetical military action: "Blue forces (the enemy) coming from the south are to be found 'strongly' entrenched on *Snail Hill.*"

The text of the tactical exercise continued for more than twenty pages, single-spaced. Due to the competitive nature of the generals, the key word in this argument was "strongly." One of the generals, "Screwball" Briones (who represented the enemy) wanting to win the battle, wished it to mean the following: "concrete bunkers with land mines planted at the foot of the hill." The commander of the Peruvian "Red Forces," "Casper"[6] De La Piedra (just as equally desirous of achieving a triumphant victory over his comrade) thought that it meant, "Ditches, dug four feet deep in the sand, of undetermined length, but capped at both ends with rolls of barbed wire."

While these generals argued their disparate points of view, supporting their theories with the coarsest of epithets, little by little, the cadets were falling asleep in their humble foxholes. As they lay there with their childlike faces on the sandy plain, at the foot of Raven Hill, where their hot-under-the-collar generals quarreled, the artillery cadets, operating the mortars fifteen hundred feet behind the generals' command post, also slumbered deeply under the Sandman's spell. When one of the commanders finally arrived at a Solomonic agreement with his counterpart: "Concrete trenches and two lines of barbed wire obstacles," the order

---

[6] His nickname referred to the fact that he resembled, head to toe, the "Friendly Ghost."

to "FIRE!" was transmitted via the field radio. The brusqueness of this authoritarian expression startled an artillery cadet who was cradling, half way inside the barrel, the body of an unfired mortar shell. Cadet Solícito Mundaca awoke, choking on, and spitting out, a fly that had landed in his half-open mouth while he was nodding off. Stumbling about, he accidentally changed the trajectory of the mortar when his knee hit the steel tube and he let go of the object that he was holding in his hands.

When one fires a mortar, the sound it makes isn't very loud. To anyone standing nearby, it sounds more like someone slapping the end of an empty ten-foot sewer PVC pipe, or popping the cork of a gigantic bottle of champagne; however, the explosion of a one-hundred-twenty-millimeter mortar shell is an entirely different matter. The Second Lieutenant, Gerardo Arrieta, is aware of the difference between the two, because on that day, as a "Cow[7]", he had been sleeping peacefully at the foot of Raven Hill, his face covered with his *blessed* steel helmet, when that mortar shell exploded some forty-five feet from him. The blast occurred while the two generals were still arguing bitterly at the top of the hill.

Arrieta awoke. At first, he didn't know if it was because of the noise that sounded like a deafening thunderclap, or because of the brutal force with which a horseshoe-shaped piece of shrapnel knocked the helmet off his face, and ended up encrusted in Cadet Ligurio's pelvis. Seconds before, Rigoberto "Beto" Ligurio, wanting to win a wager with another cadet in the foxhole to the right of him, had stood up to piss on the stomach of his neighbor to the left, who was pleasantly snoring. The maneuvers ended because of an order issued by the two generals, who had reached an agreement to do so, exactly two minutes after the accident.

---

[7] A third-year cadet in a US military academy; in Peru, he is called *Aspirante* (Aspirant).

* * *

Rigoberto Ligurio received medical treatment in the United States of America under the auspices of the Department of Defense. This evacuation was unusual, but possible thanks to the fact that these maneuvers fell under the special category of "Continental Defense."

The most renowned specialists in the U.S. fought in vain to reattach Rigoberto's penis. Henceforth, "Stubby" Ligurio received a life-long pension both as compensation for his painful loss and for his actions "beyond the call of duty." As for Cadet Arrieta, he received a severe punishment for his imprudent action of sleeping on his back, with his helmet on his face, during a live-fire exercise. Furthermore, for an extended period, he saw himself forced to use prescription eardrops, surreptitiously acquired from the academy's infirmary, until his hearing came back and the pain stopped.

AT THE BREAK OF DAWN

Hilario, that man whom many believed to be a demon incarnate, furiously noticed how a cold draft entered his home through a small gap between the threshold and the bottom of the main door. Pouncing like a cat on the problem, he tried to contain the icy breeze, but it was too late; the frigid air had already ensconced itself in the dirt floor of his room.

$$* \quad * \quad *$$

Yatiri, the old medicine man of Ninantaya, envisioned Hilario's house. He could see in his mind's eye the blast of wind that he conjured up, coursing through the aperture in the front door. It was the first time in his life that Yatiri found it difficult to swallow. The curandero pricked his ears and listened to the crackling rust on the door's hinges. "We'll see about this, '*cholito*', son of Satan," he muttered. "You dared to challenge my authority by trying to kill my protégé, Second Lieutenant Arrieta. Now, let's see how you get out of this trap that I prepared for you!"

The Aimara witch doctor then chuckled as he remembered the days that followed Hilario's attack upon the second lieutenant. He knows that that Indian almost broke the officer's right leg, with a fragrant eucalyptus branch that he always carried with him. That event took place on a clear night, while the young officer was looking up at the stars in the front yard of his house.

* * *

"No one can kill me," Hilario said suddenly, sitting in his straw chair, "many have tried, but I've always prevailed, just like my father prophesied when I was a child." He mumbled gruffly while studying his sallow complexion in a small mirror shard that hung on the wall next to him. "Nobody will kill me," he murmured. "My destiny is to live on. It's written that no one will have the power to kill me." He pondered this profoundly, and it showed on his face. "No one on earth is even able to look me in the eyes," he added, sniffling hard and slurping his phlegm, before spitting a large green gob, as far as he could. Then, he smiled calmly.

Hilario's house was a set of empty rooms saturated with the odor of rotten meat. In the last room of this dwelling, there were an iron-framed bed covered with recently flayed alpaca hides; two kerosene lamps in the middle of the floor; and a line of cudgels of various sizes, propped up against a wall like baseball bats. On the nightstand, right next to the bed, one could see two antique revolvers still in good working order and an open box of ammunition with the cartridges sticking out half way.

* * *

The residents of the fiefdom of Ninantaya[8] went to bed very late the last three nights of the month. They had

---

[8] The Spanish subdivided all the land in the Altiplano under the feudal system that they imported to the New World in this manner.

decided to gather in the plaza at dusk, in front of their dilapidated, priest-less church, to discuss, in hushed voices, what's happening between Hilario, the son of Satan, and Yatiri, the man whom everyone knew to be a man of God. "Well, Yatiri cures our diseases; that's for sure. He brings us good harvests and he makes the rain come when we need it," said every man present, one after the other, as if the words were the meeting's chosen mantra. "As for Hilario, well, it's best not to talk about him," said the Indians. "He likes to take lives just for the fun of it," declared one of them. "I've seen him kill a lamb with his bare hands," stated another, "he reached his fingers inside the belly of the animal to rip out its heart. Then, he ate it while it was still beating, hot and steaming."

Suddenly, everyone heard a noise that frightened them as they sensed a blurry figure had zip past under their very noses. They felt a cold shiver crawl up their spines and they ran back to their houses like frightened vizcachas fleeing from a predator they've not seen, but somehow sense that he is coming.

* * *

Second Lieutenant Arrieta vomited repeatedly over the starboard side of the naval patrol boat. His friend, First Lieutenant Losada, gave him a piece of dry bread and told him to chew tiny bits of it. "So that you'll have something to puke up," he said in a low voice. Young Arrieta breathed deeply and then he doubled over again as his abdominal muscles contracted and forced him to empty the contents of his stomach once more. Though briefly wrapped up in his retching, the second lieutenant jumped up when the boat's commander let him know that they had arrived and that it was time to step onto dry land. Arrieta, wearing black combat fatigues, checked over his equipment, touching each item with his fingertips. On the right side of his belt, he carried his nine-millimeter pistol. He also had two knives, one sheathed on his left side and the other tucked in the small of his back. Hanging from his bandolier, was a long and thin iron tube that looked like a rifle barrel peeking out of a cloth wrap. "With that tube, you could chop a Christian in half," said the naval officer steering the boat. "Or a leg at least," Arrieta answered back, cracking a smile. A thick strap wrapped around his waist held leather bags filled with bullets for his pistol. "Get your lazy ass going," said Lieutenant Losada, "I don't have a lot of time to waste and you're going to delay your visit." As Gerardo Arrieta ambled towards the beach, he felt the icy sting of the frigid waters that drenched his shins, calves, and knees. He could hear his legs brushing up against the leaves of the *totora*[9], the murmur of the small waves curling over to lap the dry sand of the beach…and he became lost in thought.

He recalled how, after having completed his eventful and unfortunate six-month posting in the FOB Ninantaya, he returned to his main operating base in Otábala. He knew that he should have gotten over it by now, but despite surviving so many of the awful things that happened to him in Otábala, one after another he found himself reliving them in his mind. He couldn't believe what he discovered. Junior officers full of testosterone, clandestinely satisfying the wives of senior officers; high-ranking officers stealing the food of both their troops and their horses; incredible stock shortages found in the depots put under his care by his superiors; and finally, Yatiri's ghostly apparition startling him while he was enveloped in the darkness of one of those storehouses. The old man came out of nowhere; a gray, penitent soul demanding that Arrieta fulfill his destiny by killing Hilario. "Remember; two shots in cross formation, one in the temple and the other in the forehead. And be careful, second lieutenant; they got to be good, clean shots,

---

[9] A kind of reed that grows in the shores of Lake Titicaca.

papitooo," Yatiri had said. Then the medicine man disappeared back into the dark from whence he came.

Arrieta recalled that the old man had pulled the same vanishing act and given him a similar set of instructions when he had taken him by the hand from Ninantaya to Umuchi. "Yes!" the young officer said, "It's almost as if it had happened yesterday; I went to Umuchi with Yatiri, while I was lying in bed trying to recover from that damn leg injury."

As dangerous as the curandero's request might have appeared, Gerardo Arrieta was a great soldier, and so, during his stay in Otábala, he meditated a lot before finally coming up with a good alibi for this "secret mission." His cover story, which no one at his MOB suspected, was that he had to go to Lima because of a family emergency.

When Losada and Arrieta arrived on the other shore, Yatiri, who appeared to be nothing more than a frail, elderly man, was sitting on a boulder, waiting for them. The old man was digging through his pouch made of vicuña wool in search of the best coca leaves. His cheeks were so puffy that the skin shone like the shimmering reflection of the moon on the surface of Lake Titicaca. Yatiri, being a medicine man, passed both of his hands over his own entire body. "Tonight, you're going to receive a visitor, you wicked little *cholo*[10]," he repeated every now and then with a sharp voice, as if he were a spoiled child who was throwing a tantrum. "I'm Destiny's Overseer in this region," said the old man. "If your father, the Devil, protects you; then God, our beloved Father, watches over me," he added, seasoning his words with a flourish of hand gestures, jumps and pirouettes in mid-air. "Oh, Second Lieutenant *Arrietaaa,*" he said upon seeing the young officer, decked out like a Christmas tree. He was sporting

---

[10] Cholo(a) is a term used in Peru that primarily refers to a person who is of mixed Indian and White ancestry. The word can be used either as an insult, or as a term of endearment, even among White people.

40

knives, pistols, and a bag upon his shoulders as he emerged from between the waves of the immense lake. "I will carry you on my back, and run along the shore like a wounded deer," said the old man. "Then I will drop you off on the beach, just behind the house of that bad man to whom you must pay a visit."

* * *

All the locals, in every village on the eastern shore of Lake Titicaca, take pains to stay out of Hilario's way. They know that the Indian handles the traffic of illegal goods between Bolivia and Peru. But they also understand that the real boss in charge of the thugs steering those contraband carrying speedboats is a man whom they call the "Ghost." This man's house is in the town of Umuchi, and from there he rules the region. However, the locals fear Hilario even more. "Well, we guess it's because everyone says that he's the son of the Devil," say the communities' elders, as a standard reply, in all the lakeside villages. "He kills at least two men every night," overstate the women when they gather on the shores every day to wash the *chuño*[11] that they boil in their soup. And so on.

* * *

Hilario took off the red *chullo*[12], which he always wore, and felt how the cold breeze that invaded his house, slowly

---

[11] A small freeze-dried potato produced by the traditional Aimara process of directly exposing these tubers, in an alternating manner, to the extreme cold temperatures of the Altiplano by night and the extreme heat of the sun by day.

[12] A pointy hat with earflaps that is worn by the inhabitants of the Andes and the Altiplano and is made from the wool of either llamas, alpacas, vicuñas, or sheep.

produced in him a nervous depression. His cognitive ability diminished. His enthusiasm for evil languished. His once voracious appetite dwindled and, without him being aware of it, became a sharp pain in the pit of his stomach. As the hours wore on, his fighting spirit gave way to a nuisance. It was something that he couldn't put his finger on. He didn't know what caused it, whether it was a suffocating drowsiness, or a splitting headache, but he eventually made the drastic decision of going to sleep. This conviction of his, that sleep would uplift his mood, was the dawning of his doom. Hilario found himself trapped by Morpheus' arms, despite that his father had given him certain signs which he, irresponsibly, decided to ignore.

Earlier that evening, Hilario had heard six thunderclaps, which came from the same direction, yet he, like the rest of the townspeople, preferred to think that it was just going to rain very hard. Furthermore, he saw two black cats fighting two white cats in front of his house. The white cats won, and Hilario kicked the black cats as punishment for their poor performance. The most ominous sign, however, was the sudden death of a slate colored coot, with a bright red crest, at the back of his house. He ignored this completely. Hilario paid no heed to the harsh reality that one can't put too much trust in supernatural protection, even if one were to assume that his own father was the most important figure second to God Himself.

* * *

The people of Umuchi talked for days and weeks in the town square about how Hilario found himself to be the victim of a horrible crime. They said that the Indian had received a strange visitor before the break of dawn on Easter Sunday. The town's matrons put their hands on their heads, took hold of their long hair and braided the strands over

42

their eyes upon commenting on the twisted nature of the criminals who paid Hilario a visit. "Can you believe it, *comadre*[13]? What crazy idea would drive someone to commit the sin of killing a man on the very day our Lord rose from the dead?" Then, the town baker mentioned that he was friends with a corporal in the Rural Civil Guard.

"How did they kill him, *señorcitoooo*?" one of the matrons asked.

"My friend, the police corporal," said the bread maker, "told me that the victim's left femur was broken in half. That he had a bullet hole in the left temple with an exit wound on the right side, and a large hole in the middle of his forehead," the *panadero*[14] explained, using his hands to illustrate on his own head where the gendarme had found the injuries. Finally, the parish priest appeared on the scene, making the sign of the cross repeatedly. He added that Hilario's execution was religious in nature, or perhaps had something to do with the witchcraft business, because the perpetrator had made the bullet holes in the shape of a cross, and that, according to some people, is how one should kill a man who is possessed by a demon. "The murderer must have come from far away," concluded the priest. "No man in this town would have had the guts to confront Hilario, much less try to kill him."

* * *

Yatiri, Second Lieutenant Arrieta, and his friend, the naval lieutenant Losada, were drinking *cañazo* in a cantina close to the port of Puno. They didn't allow anyone to come within a hundred feet of them, but from far away one could see that they were ecstatic and were celebrating some sort

---

[13] A Spanish term used by a woman in either referring to, or addressing, her child's godmother.
[14] Spanish for someone who makes and sells bread.

of victory. They drank and chewed on coca leaves throughout the night. At the break of dawn, they went their separate ways. As they were walking, all three of them raised their hands and waved good-bye to each other. Yatiri returned to Ninantaya, the fiefdom where he lived, a few leagues to the south of Umuchi. Arrieta returned to his MOB in Otábala, to the south of the lake. And the navy lieutenant, caressing in his pocket his orders for a new assignment, returned to the capital city of Lima, a place that takes several hours to get to by airplane.

ELEODORO & VIRGINIA

The rider sensed his horse's strength, agility, and obedience, as he had never felt it before. Eleodoro Irigoyen sat astride the animal and tried to appear composed as he concentrated on the obstacle course that lay ahead of him. General Irigoyen knew very well that his wife was sitting in the stands and was observing him anxiously. It was then that he felt the hairs on the back of his neck stand on end as he pondered the possibility of an accident. Falling off his horse was something that had never occurred to him, but at his age... "That's when the years begin to take their toll," he thought. He shook off those doubts and, without wasting any more time, focused on the first obstacle. Nothing else mattered. As he approached the brush fence, courage welled up inside him. It always happened that way. The anxiety and the stomach cramps one felt before the competition disappeared after the first jump.

*   *   *

Cadet Arrieta, a patient in the orthopedic wing of the military hospital, rolled his wheel chair along the main hallway. He advanced without making any sounds, apart from the occasional chirping of the chair's rubber wheels against the gleaming tiled floor. All those people in search of medical attention left many hours ago. Most of the doctors attended patients until two in the afternoon and it was already seven o'clock at night. The young man with a crew cut continued rolling down the hall until he reached the elevator. He pressed the call button and parked his chair facing the elevator door. He turned his head to the left and contemplated the back of a nurse walking down the corridor under the pale fluorescent recessed lights.

The man whom Arrieta was looking to visit was in an awful situation. "It's a severe case of quadriplegia," said the neurosurgeon, Dr. Nieves. He explained in detail to the inquisitive Firstie[15] in the wheelchair that, "when the fracture occurs at the height of the cervical vertebrae and the spine is damaged, one is only able to move the lips and the tongue." The doctor said this in a composed manner, and recommended that Arrieta avoid conversations about this topic, with his friend the general.

Once inside the elevator, and immersed in a mist pregnant with the smell of a strong antiseptic, the cadet began to sweat. He wiped his hands on the lap of his pajama bottoms and combed his short hair with his palms. Both the discipline and the norms of the military academy, had so thoroughly subdued his mind that he could not enter any room without worrying about looking acceptable.

As the floor indicator light for the second floor lit up, with the usual "ding," and the elevator door opened, he wheeled out to the right and rolled down the corridor leading to the hospital's south wing. His heart began to beat like a hand gallop; its rhythm was energetic, yet controlled by a set of reins that were much too tense. This is the point at which the horse appears to be galloping in one place and his chest, as well as the sides of his neck, starts to sweat foam. Steeped in this state of agitation, Arrieta's mind raced to

---

[15] Term used in US military academies for cadets in their fourth and last year; in Peru, he is called *Técnico* (Technician).

come up with the proper greeting to use upon reaching the room of the patient about whom he was so concerned.

* * *

Virginia retrieved a compact from her purse. She opened it with ease and studied the reflection of her face in its small oval mirror. She took her lipstick from her hand purse and, with it, carefully touched up the contours of her full, plump lips. A startled, muted "Oh!" from the crowd, tore her from her reverie. She looked at the jump track in front of her and contemplated the rider, wrapped up in the shame of having to remount, after he'd fallen off his horse when it refused to hurdle a wall. "This is what happens most of the time," her husband Eleodoro had explained to her, in diverse occasions. "I don't know why those quadrupeds have such a problem calculating the height of the wall. It wouldn't hurt them to jump a few feet beforehand; then everything would be just fine," Eleodoro would say each time he saw a horse violently and unexpectedly shift to one side of a wall and resist the order to jump.

* * *

Gerardo Arrieta vividly remembers, as if it were a dream, the Sunday when he first met Eleodoro Irigoyen. At the time, Arrieta was still a Pleb[16] and it had become the norm for him to be placed on restriction and consequently lose his weekend privileges. His irascible temperament and free spirit had driven him down a dead-end street: it seemed that he would never be able to see the world outside the

---

[16] Term used in US military academies to refer to cadets in their first year; in Peru, they are called, *Perro* (Dog).

walls of the academy. But, he had already become used to this. He enjoyed any opportunity for merriment that presented itself during his periods of restriction.

One Sunday, the Officer of the Day sent him to help set up tables and chairs at the officer's club, hours before they were going to host a party. It was there that the then-Colonel Eleodoro Irigoyen was with his beautiful wife. Everyone had spoken to him about this fine couple, praising the unique woman who was the colonel's companion. Arrieta saw her and concluded that she was much more beautiful than he had imagined at first; however, he was unable to guess her age accurately. The colonel's conduct and his way of speaking with those around him, gave the impression that he'd spent a few years at this rank.

After doing the math in his head, Arrieta concluded that the man was somewhere between fifty and fifty-five years old. She, on the other hand, appeared to be between twenty-three and twenty-eight years old. Despite this, the cadet thought that this woman could easily be seen going out with a man his own age, a kid of just eighteen years old. Irigoyen's wife looked like a beauty queen. The texture of her skin was impressive. Her muscles were firm and solid like those of an Olympic athlete. Of course, she was an assiduous tennis player, but even then, her beauty seemed to be more innate than acquired. Arrieta did his best to help set up for the party at the Officer's Club, but all the while, he couldn't stop thinking about the age disparity between the two members of that marital union. At the end, what he saw and heard convinced him that those two were truly in love and lived for each other.

* * *

After the brush fence, which was easy to clear, Eleodoro went for an ascending 'oxer', a triple bar oxer, and a roll top. The horse hadn't even finished landing its back hooves well enough on the ground, after jumping over a water ditch, when General Irigoyen pulled hard on the left reign and made a sharp turn in a short amount of space. The public attending the Cavalry Day celebration kept the customary silence so as not to spook the animal.

Coming out of the last curve, Irigoyen faced the awe-inspiring wall, an obstacle of almost five feet. He stared at the wall and understood that even though he wasn't afraid, the fact that other people were watching him made this obstacle look much larger than it was. Eleodoro thought about Virginia, his twenty-eight-year old wife, and a turbulent flush of emotion invaded him without respite. He imagined her in the stands, well dressed to highlight her alluring frame, and made up like a movie star to show off her beauty and her nymph-like face.

*   *   *

When Arrieta reached the room's entrance, he could see the patient sitting in a high-back wheelchair. The timid light of the lamp on the nightstand let the cadet notice that the individual was so well dressed that it made one feel sorry for him. His paralysis and his helplessness were aggressively obvious. The quadriplegic, sitting up and appearing composed, maintained his position with the help of seven transparent plastic straps. The first of these wrapped around his forehead, keeping it elevated. The second was rather loose and wrapped around his neck, just under his jawbone. A third strap, which was thicker than the rest, passed across his chest and looped around under both armpits. Both forearms rested on the armrests forming a right angle at the elbows, with each wrist held by leather restraints. Lastly, there were two belts fastening the lower legs, just below the knees where the tibia and fibula join.

As he crossed the threshold of the half-opened door, the cadet caught a whiff of a familiar scent. It was the perfume worn by the patient's wife. This aroma always permeated the room. The wife made sure to spray it when she was there during the day. However, over the past few months, the fragrance became contaminated, and that night Arrieta smelled an entirely different odor. The invalid wore diapers underneath his underwear and he would urinate in them freely. Anything that he drank, he would drain out of his bladder in a matter of minutes. The pungency of the odor depended very much on the quality of care given by the nurses. If they failed to change him over time, the acidity of the perfume increased and whoever came into the room at that moment would have to try hard to get used to it.

The smell of the room depended on the time of the day. After 6pm, it reeked of ammonia and decomposed bacteria found in urine. During the mornings, when the nurses bathed him and facilitated the functioning of his bowel movements, the stench of excrement was overwhelming. This was the tragic and exasperating reality of that patient.

* * *

Virginia closed her eyes when Eleodoro spurred his horse at a gallop to jump the wall. Seconds later, she heard the horrified crowd in the stands gasp a collective "OH!" and she shut her eyelids even tighter. She somehow wanted to escape the reality of what just happened, and, curiously, at that moment, her thoughts raced back in time to when she first met Eleodoro Irigoyen.

"If I were younger, say ten years younger, would you go out with me?" Eleodoro Irigoyen asked a girl dressed all in white without giving her back the tennis ball that he picked up from the clay floor. The young woman eyed the man from top to bottom, smiled broadly, and reached out her hand.

With a wiggle of her nimble fingers, she laid claim to the ball without saying a word. Eleodoro's face turned beet-red as he stammered out a clumsy apology. He sensed a hot wave rising from the pit of his stomach to the top of his head and, with his hand still stretched out, thought for a moment that he was going to faint.

Upon witnessing this miracle, the woman dressed in white, with a tennis racket in her hand and a tennis ball in the pocket of her skirt, let out a girlish laugh before taking Eleodoro's frozen hand into hers. "You're as tender as a child," she told him. "The last time any boy approached me in that way was in high school." The young woman then continued talking and quite naturally interlocked her right arm with his left as they both began to make their way to the clubhouse restaurant "I'm not afraid of you," she said as she placed her tennis racket on a table. "My father died a general."

Colonel Irigoyen walked with her without saying a word and every step of the way he marveled that he was with her. "You don't need to be younger to go out with me," said the girl as she felt his bicep with her free hand. "Do you work out a lot?" she asked with childlike wonder while squeezing his arm. Eleodoro remained quiet until they reached the restaurant's front door. There a jovial, elderly employee in a dark-colored uniform welcomed them. "Come inside, Colonel," he said as he opened the door with a bow. Upon encountering the maître d', an old acquaintance of his, Eleodoro composed himself. He straightened out the arm the young woman was clinging and used the other one to invite her to enter before him. He wanted to demonstrate his good upbringing and especially, his profound respect for her.

Arrieta entered the room and wheeled his chair to where the General could see him face to face. Once he managed to get his friend's attention, they exchanged pleasantries that evolved into an aggressive inquiry on the part of the older patient.

The quadriplegic lost patience with his condition. As a result, he began to vent his frustration, launching into bitter diatribes against the young man who had visited him every night for the last few weeks. He behaved unacceptably towards the cadet in compensation for the false optimism and faith in the signs of recovery he had to show to his wife every day that she came to visit. He constantly pretended for her that soon he was going to be able to walk again, be the man of the house, and play with their young children in their backyard.

Arrieta's crippled friend liked to use a striking metaphor that he came up with to describe himself: "Here, sitting before you, young man, is a head attached to a flower pot." The General went on to speculate about his own sad reality, dramatizing with the crudest of words the details of his daily activities.

Eleodoro and Virginia crossed the floor of the great dining hall and went directly to the bar. The colonel ordered a soda for the young woman and a whisky for himself. "In a tall glass with ice and mineral water...you know how I like it, Ernesto," he told the man behind the bar. Virginia slapped the bar's dark shiny wood top like a cowboy in a saloon and demanded, "I'll have mine on the rocks, Ernesto...you also know how I like it!" Then, she beamed a wide and irresistible smile.

Eleodoro apologized for not asking whether she wanted ice, mumbled incoherently for a few seconds, and then stared at Virginia like someone looking at an apparition. Despite their short time together, he already appeared to be very much in love. He sighed out of an intense feeling of joy and foreboding; he had surrendered unto her unconditionally.

Virginia returned his gaze, moved towards him, and, with the fingers of her right hand, parted the hairs resting on his forehead. She did this with such innocence and tenderness that Ernesto, the maître d,' smilingly became part of this triptych of contemplation as he arrived with the couples' drinks. "I love whisky; but I'm not an alcoholic," said Eleodoro. "Me also," quipped Virginia, "I'll have a few drinks from time to time. Not much...just two or three...it depends on the occasion," she cleared up, with a hearty laugh.

* * *

"I feel nothing from the neck down," said the man in the high-back wheel chair, almost yelling. "This is what I call 'the flower pot.' The nurses come in the morning and bathe me. Next, they literally force the shit out of my guts by squeezing the area where my intestines happened to be. The smell that follows these massages is unbearable; it makes me want to puke. As you can imagine, cadet, the shame I feel because of this is demoralizing and I'm beginning to detest the existence of all those around me; especially my own!" Tears streamed down his face. There followed a silence of many seconds before he continued. "After they clean and wash me, they massage my legs and ass. Can you believe that? And I can't feel a damn thing. It's as if they were working on someone else's body," he said in a calm demeanor once he had recovered his composure. "This is life without living, my dear cadet," he mumbled before releasing a heavy sigh. Arrieta's friend repeated this last phrase incessantly, intensifying and expanding the gravity of his depression, making it even more fatal. "I want to kill myself," he said suddenly with a choking voice. The young man in the wheel chair was startled to hear this. "Yes, damn it! I want someone with enough balls to help me cease to exist!"

* * *

Virginia had three children. To the delight of her husband, all of them were boys, and they had had one for every year they were married. Eleodoro was a dedicated and reliable husband. She named her three boys, in one way or another, after their father. The firstborn was Eleodoro Jorge, Gerardo Eleodoro was the second, and Dionisio Eleodoro was the third. After Dionisio was born, the couple decided to stop adding on to their family because Virginia's gynecologist discovered that she had a slight heart murmur. "It's so insignificant that it really doesn't bother me," said this disciple of Galen with a straight face, "but I would prefer that your wife no longer have any more children. The trauma of giving birth again could turn this insignificance into something fatal."

Right away, Eleodoro responded that three, was the perfect number. He was happy with his three sons. After they left the doctor's office, he confided in his wife about a decision that he'd made a while back. Eleodoro wanted her to know that if, at any moment, someone was to ask him to give up his life to save hers he wouldn't hesitate to surrender it for not even a fraction of a second. "You've given me so much happiness over these past years that I consider my time with you to be worth a lifetime of happiness for any mere mortal such as myself."

* * *

Arrieta was alarmed. He began to think that things were getting out of hand for his quadriplegic friend. "He is not actually asking me to kill him, is he?" He thought, and as he swallowed that speculation, he felt a shiver down his spine.

Evidently, the General sensed his friend's alarm, because the quadriplegic changed the topic. "Within the drawer of that small cabinet, the nurse keeps her latex gloves," he said in a hurry. "They're the kind that surgeons use to operate," he explained. "Take out a pair, put them on, and do it without any questions. Save me the effort, dear friend. Consider my precarious situation," he exhorted. Arrieta froze. He was pinned into a corner. He didn't know what to say, or ask. He opened the drawer, removed a pair of gloves, and put them on, "without doubting or murmuring," he muttered. He raised both hands up to his eyes with his fingers pointing upwards and he felt extremely awkward. "There is a bottle under my bed. Stick your hand in there and bring it out," said the general as if he were asking for his medicine and was completely unaware that he had asked the cadet to put on the gloves.

The young man struggled to stand up. He bent over as best as he could to look under the bed. He found the bottle, short and fat, and took it out. Arrieta was very surprised. He had in his hands an unopened bottle of Chivas Regal. He didn't know what to do. It didn't occur to him to sit back down in his wheelchair. Sensing the cadet's bewilderment, the General fell back on his years of experience and went on the attack. To reinforce his will to die, he spoke non-stop. "Give me a shot, please," he implored with his voice cracking. "It's now or never," he said, without letting up, and continued with his verbal diarrhea, until Arrieta, at last convinced that he should do what the old man was

55

demanding of him, sat back down in his wheel chair, and asked him: "So, where am I supposed to get ice and mineral water around here?"

Irigoyen clarified that, given the circumstances under which they lived and considering that both he and Arrieta were patients in a hospital, there was no choice but to drink the liquor straight. "Give me a drink for the sake of charity," he insisted. Arrieta took a straw from the nightstand, put it in his friend's glass of whiskey and held it to his mouth. At that moment, he noticed that the patient's eyes were trying to draw his attention to the red bulb syringe on the nightstand. The cadet looked at both the general and the plastic object on the small table. "Can't you breathe?" he asked. The old man told him to stop being stupid; he didn't want to drown, he wanted to get drunk and pass on to the next life. "Let me remind you Cadet, that if I start to choke on that shitty phlegm that fills up my chest, you should do exactly what the nurse was doing when you came into my room last night. That way, once you have cleaned out this miserable tube, we'll be able to continue drinking. Remember, once we start drinking, we won't stop until we've finished the bottle." He was exacting in his order.

"And another thing: you are not to take off those gloves for any reason, until you get back to your room. Do you fully understand me, cadet?"

* * *

Virginia socialized with her girlfriends every day. They got together at about ten in the morning to drink coffee and chat. They took turns hosting these daily meetings and these women were married to military men.

One day, the gathering took place in the home of Veronica, an eighteen-year-old girl who had been married to a recently commissioned second lieutenant for no more than six months. That morning, Virginia was the first to arrive. After handing her a cup of coffee, Veronica offered Virginia a cigarette and lit it for her. She then lit one for herself, filled her lungs with smoke, and asked Virginia abruptly, "How were you able to marry a man who's so much older than you?" Virginia smiled, enjoyed a mouthful of smoke, and answered that Eleodoro was a marvelous man. He had the outlook and vigor of a twenty-one-year-old and her hips hurt every day from the passionate sex they had the previous night. "Every day!" she stressed. "What's more," said Virginia, "Eleodoro gets on his horse and races it almost every week. See? Now that's a strong man!"

The cadet considered that if that was what his friend truly wanted, then he had to help him. Nonetheless, he decided to make one last attempt to dissuade him. "Haven't you thought about how your wife would feel?" he asked. The General responded, very naturally, that from the beginning of his relationship with his wife, he let her know that if one day it was necessary for him to cease to exist to preserve her happiness, her general wellbeing, or even her life, then he wouldn't hesitate to die for her.

During the last three weeks, Arrieta had felt such profound compassion for his friend that, after hearing that answer, he came to find the logic in his request. "*Salud*," he said to the quadriplegic before drinking another half glass of whisky.

"It's the hospital director, mommy," said the child still in his pajamas, waving the telephone in his hand as if it were a signal flag. "It's a call for the general's wife," added the little boy. Virginia ran from the kitchen, pinning her hair back with a pair of hairpins. She took the telephone and answered hastily, "Yes, I am the wife of General Irigoyen."

The doctor informed her that her husband didn't survive the night. "During her rounds, the floor's head nurse reported, at four in the morning, that your husband passed away, apparently in his sleep," he said before becoming silent. Virginia responded calmly, "Eleodoro has been suffering, a lot, for quite some time. I am relieved that my husband can now rest in peace. His life was pure hell." She then tried to coordinate, with the person on the phone, the necessary steps that she would have to take, but the hospital director interrupted her. "Ma'am, we found an empty bottle of Chivas Regal on the nightstand. We must investigate what happened. We need to determine who is responsible, Mrs. Irigoyen," the director explained before becoming silent once more.

Virginia answered that her husband, a very active man before the accident, had played, for the past three months, the part of a living corpse. "Try to understand that the humiliation he endured, day after day, was breaking my heart. Now, I wish to bury him and honor his memory by educating his sons in the same way he would have done. And as far as the whisky is concerned, I want to make it clear, doctor, that my husband and I enjoyed drinking it," she said, hanging up the phone without waiting for any response.

* * *

The nurse knocked on the door of Cadet Arrieta's room and asked, two or three times, if he was "decent."

The Firstie's eyes lit up like a pair of flashlights. He then stretched out his right hand and immediately searched for the tube of toothpaste that he had on top of his nightstand. Upon grabbing a hold of it he repeated the same maneuver he executed the previous night, right after he got back from the General's room. He uncapped the tube and squirted a gob of toothpaste into his mouth. Swishing it around for thirty seconds before swallowing, he quickly tossed the tube of toothpaste into his nightstand drawer, and laid back down on his bed, saying, "Yes, ma'am, I'm decent enough for you." To which the nurse replied, "Young man, if you're naked, I'm going to take you straight to the hospital director's office; so, don't play games with me, sonny." She then entered the room, pushing an empty wheelchair, as if to suggest the cadet should jump into it. He did so and she asked him, "Are you ready for your hydrotherapy treatment?" He said, "Yes, ma'am; I'm always ready for a beautiful lady."

As they made their way to the hospital's physical therapy room, they both continued conversing just as they did every morning. He asked her if she slept well last night. She answered no. Then, she said that someone had killed General Irigoyen last night. Arrieta became pale. His nerves began to act up in such a way that he even slightly wet his pajama bottoms. The sky-blue poplin of his pants evinced a dark circle just below his fly.

"How...? Who? Where?" stammered Arrieta. The nurse informed him that some irresponsible murderer had given the general some whisky to drink and in such copious quantity, that the old man became intoxicated, lost all consciousness, and then, shortly thereafter, died. Cadet Arrieta, fixing his eyes on his feet, mumbled that he'd heard the general say on multiple occasions that he preferred death to continuing the sort of life that he was leading, that he was asking for someone with enough courage to help him to die decently, that he wanted to leave this Earth on his own terms.

The cadet heard a sharp buzz in his ears. He covered them with both hands and closed his eyes. Within his head resonated, full blast and with a metallic echo, the words Irigoyen had spoken as Arrieta showed him the empty bottle which the two of them had just downed without any restraint or remorse. "One fucking second changed it all! Just one second makes all the difference," the patient had shouted with a broken voice, but without shedding a single tear. "For fuck's sake, cadet! Stop crying!" the General added, when he saw tears streaming down his friend's cheeks.

"I was thrown out of my saddle when my horse planted himself in front of the wall. As I went flying, I could hear the sound that the wind makes as it crashes against the folds of the outer ear. I fell feet first on the soft grass of the jump course, but the determination I had in my mind to remain that way, upright and in control of my movements, was just an ephemeral idea that my body, for no valid reason I could think of, didn't know how to execute. It must be my age," sighed the general and, in his eyes, one could see the anguish caused by a shortness of breath. The cadet then took the red bulb syringe that he had used several times before and, with his recently acquired dexterity, he extracted the pestilent phlegm inhabiting the catheter that protruded out of his friend's chest. The general breathed deeply many times, and as he did so one could hear, the gurgling sound produced by air mixed with mucus. Afterwards, he continued to speak. "I started to fall towards the ground, and I had nothing to cushion my fall. As I approached the grass with all my humanity, I recalled some of my combat experience and I managed to turn my body in such a way that would help me touch down and roll over until I could end up on the grass in a horizontal position.

"I felt my leg gently touch the ground; then my knee, thigh, hip, elbow, arm, and shoulder. And just when I was feeling satisfied about my perfect landing, and I was almost ready to declare victory because I thought that the next things to touch the grass were going to be my ear, and my head, there came the gruesome surprise. I sensed something cracking inside my neck; something like a branch ripped apart from the trunk of a tree. One second, cadet! Just one second makes all the difference. As a result, my dear friend, my body turned into a flowerpot."

Arrieta asked the nurse if the general had choked to death. She answered, no. "He just stopped breathing," she explained. Yet, once they reached the rehabilitation room, the nurse declared with a triumphant air, "but they're going to find the one responsible for this tragedy. It's only a matter of days, no more. And you can rest assured, cadet," she said assuming the tone of a high court judge, "that when they find him, they're going to put him in jail for murder."

Then, the nurse whispered to him: "They've already taken the empty bottle and the glass to see if they can lift any fingerprints from them."

DESTINY'S OVERSEER

Yatiri, the medicine man of Ninantaya, says that to kill a demon incarnate one needs to have both a firm hand and absolute conviction. Although he knows that this is not his line of work, his familiarity with destiny's rugged and unchartered byways has nonetheless compelled him to design a series of schemes that will eliminate any of those hazards that life's recurrent coincidences tend to engender. Yatiri is deeply involved with the destiny of that fiefdom's inhabitants because of his dedication to helping others. "No sulfur-reeking demon, no matter how important he could be, will ever shove me out of the way," he utters between his gums. And as he fills his mouth with the coca leaves that he so carefully selected, he murmurs, "I'm going to help the second lieutenant, who's the victim of that malignant attack, so that he can take charge of his own fate."

* * *

The most powerful man in the region where the Ninantaya Hacienda is situated is a mestizo-looking individual whom the people of those environs know by the nickname "Ghost." Ninantaya is a town comprised of four houses and a church whose walls rise no higher than a llama.

These four dwellings serve as the office of the telegraph operator; the office of the civil guard, with its two gendarmes; the schoolhouse for the town's solitary teacher; and the customs house. The customs officers are two middle-aged men and the people of this small hamlet insist on stating, with a grin, that both sleep in the same bed.

The half-a-church has been in this state ever since the *taita*[17] priest bailed out on his parish some ten years ago. No one has a clear memory of what exactly happened; all they know is that the roof collapsed and the next morning the walls were in ruins. Since then, they have stayed at a height of no more than five feet. The only thing that remained intact, and standing upright, was the high altar with a rickety cross in the middle. It seems that whoever caused this destruction felt restrained by a grave fear. Or perhaps some other impediment kept him from destroying the symbols that the people of Ninantaya know to represent God Himself. Some of the older townspeople, already showing signs of senility, believe that the culprit was a certain Hilario, who people say is a reincarnated demon. However, none of the younger denizens gives this explanation any credence.

* * *

Just hearing the name of the "Ghost" is enough to startle all the inhabitants of that area except for one: the shaman, Yatiri. This old Indian, who has only three teeth, heals every townsperson who exhibits any symptoms of ill health in the body or mind. Yet, when it comes to the case of an acute infection, the Ghost sometimes interferes with the work of the old medicine man. He gives himself the satisfaction of bringing powerful, injectable antibiotics

---

[17] A term of respect used by the natives when they address authority figures (like: "My lord" in English).

from La Paz, over in Bolivia. The capital of this neighboring country is just a few hours away from Ninantaya, but one is only able to make this trip in such a short amount of time by driving there and back in a four-wheel-drive suburban like the kind the Ghost uses as his personal transport.

Whenever Yatiri witnesses these "unnatural" interventions (that is according to this old man's peculiar interpretation of reality), he simply smiles because he understands the logic of life. He knows that when someone contracts an infection and doesn't respond to his prayers and herbs it's because that person has reached the end of his time here on earth. When the Ghost chooses to partake in the realm of health care provider, Yatiri just turns around and, as he shrugs his shoulders and shakes his head in resignation, marches off with a smile upon his lips.

The Ghost, for his part, doesn't question Yatiri's behavior because he knows that the witch doctor is right. Still, he suspects that the old man's body language could mean that in bringing the antibiotics he's assuming a serious responsibility by contradicting the fate of the infected townspeople. Everyone knows that thanks to these drugs the Ghost 'imports' from Bolivia many have been brought back from the brink of death after a smiling Yatiri had given them the good news that their departure from this world was irremissible.

* * *

Yatiri is a character straight out of a storybook. He is old, very short, and possesses a skeletal body. The color of his hair is a yellowish-white mixed with black strands that give one the impression of uncleanliness. His long hair grows down to his waist and he ties it into a knot just below the back of his neck. His fingers are longer than they should be with respect to the size of his body. His lips stained with a greenish tinge advertise his ancestral habit of continuously chewing coca leaves.

Yatiri's talent for weaving is unmatched for seven leagues around. With simple wool threads, the old man can make whatever anyone asks of him. His long fingers help him to spin wool with his distaff, as well as knit with wooden needles, like no one else. But, most importantly of all, he can use his own time to practice these skills, due to his age (of which no one is certain) and his position as the resident medicine man for Ninantaya. These two attributes exempt him from the fieldwork that overwhelms almost all the inhabitants of the hacienda.

* * *

The Ghost is a forceful man with many domains, one of which is a monopoly on smuggling. To carry out this high-risk enterprise, he counts on the services provided by his nephews, the three Lara brothers. During their evening conversations over cups of canned heat[18], the people of this small hamlet gossip that the oldest one, Hilario (known by the nickname "Chullo"), is the Devil incarnate himself. Likewise, they say that the second one, Francisco, is a helpless communist who not only kills on the orders of his uncle, but also for pleasure. Regarding the third one, Germán, there is a great deal of controversy surrounding him. Most of the townspeople know the story about how his uncle put a bullet in the back of his neck. They say that on this occasion the Ghost was unable to control his temper at the former's uncommon lack of respect. Even so, almost

---

[18] Also known as "Sterno," canned heat is a fuel made from denatured and jellied alcohol which is meant to be burned directly from its can for "buffet heating" in the food catering business. In Peru, it is known as "ron de quemar."

everyone in Ninantaya believes the popular myth that Germán, despite being dead, still shows up at his uncle's house every time the Ghost needs him to do his dirty work.

* * *

Yatiri garners the respect, not only of the people of Ninantaya, but also that of the populace in the neighboring cities like Umuchi, to the north, and Puerto Acosta, to the south, in Bolivia. The people of Ninantaya also know that the shaman even has admirers in the far-off city of Rucano. The hacienda where Yatiri lives (as fate would have it) belongs to the Peruvian Army. Rumor has it that a very rich man who happened to own many latifundia bestowed this piece of land to the military because he was so tired of dealing with the armed border disputes in this region. The gravel road traversing the Ninantaya Hacienda connects Peru with Bolivia and allows the people of that region to hold a sabbatical fair in the town square. Or at least, that is the official reason for the construction of said road.

The plaza in the middle of this four-house town is a dirty windswept field, scattered with gray stones, that faces the dilapidated church. Every Saturday this town square fills with people from all around the region who come to acquire the basic groceries to meet the needs of their simple lives. The underlying reality is that this gravel road facilitates a large-scale smuggling operation into Peru from Chile's free port of Arica.

* * *

Yatiri asserts that 'Chullo' will never cross his path. Whenever an Indian asks him (usually prolonging the vowel

66

sounds at the end of each word) why '*Chullitooo*' takes care never to get in Yatiri's way, the shaman responds by saying: "it's because one of us will have to leave this world at that very *momeeent*." The only person who ever dared to ask the old man which of the two individuals would have to cease to exist, was Second Lieutenant Arrieta, the Ninantaya Hacienda's administrator. This is because the young officer was convinced that his uniform and the pistol on his belt granted him a kind of all-encompassing authority over those under his charge in the hacienda. However, over time, Arrieta came to understand that true authority comes from other qualities found in men, almost all of which have nothing to do with those of the uniform.

When the second lieutenant asked Yatiri such a seemingly overwhelming question, the old Indian laughed good-naturedly, placed his wrinkled hand on Arrieta's shoulder, and conversed with him for several hours to explain to him just how complex destiny really is.

The young officer could never comprehend, much less make others understand, how it was that the two of them were able to understand each other for such a long period even though Yatiri only spoke Aimara and he spoke only Spanish. In fact, part of Arrieta's astonishment lay in the fact that without his having ever seen the sun seek refuge behind the hills he was convinced that his conversation with the old man had lasted at least two weeks.

* * *

When 'Chullo' (or if one prefers: Hilario), assaulted the second lieutenant, things got complicated. The event became a personal affront to Yatiri. The young military officer's health was in such a critical state that he could have died. Scratching his head with his distaff, the medicine man manifested his astonishment with this attack. The shaman realized that Hilario had crossed the line without suffering any consequences. The old man knew that he would have to take decisive actions or he would risk endangering himself.

Until that day, Hilario, the man with the red chullo, had been certain that if he crossed Yatiri's path or went against the old man's plans, then at that precise moment he would have initiated the last leg of his life's journey. But nothing happened...or at least that's what 'Chullo' thought.

*   *   *

The second lieutenant sensed that someone had broken his leg at the level of his thigh and he believed that he had lost all consciousness. The young man took a turn for the worse and for several days, he was on the brink of death. Meanwhile, Yatiri was at the foot of his bed, night, and day, applying potions, oils, and herbs until he saved the young officer's life.

The Ghost silently observed the attack from far away. "This is a matter of essential respect for my rank," he told his nephews. "You shouldn't have harmed the second lieutenant without my authorization," he shouted at the oldest of them while keeping a safe distance. Hilario shrugged his shoulders and aggressively spat on the floor. The uncle shoved his hand into his coat pocket and all the men around him changed their tune. They were wary of what could happen because it was common knowledge that the Ghost carried an old Luger in that same pocket. In fact, some of the men, who could stand close enough to him, mumbled that they've seen bullet holes in that grey gabardine coat of his at the level of the right pocket.

After a brief and uncomfortable silence, the Ghost told Hilario that he was his flesh-and-blood uncle and as such, he was entitled to exercise great authority over him. And that if, in the future, he, Hilario, should decide to act on his own, he should remember that he is nothing without his uncle; that everyone, without exception, needed his uncle Tomás. "So, calm down, nephew, and think twice before acting on your own accord."

* * *

During the days that the Second Lieutenant was bedridden, Yatiri took the opportunity to mold the young officer according to his will. For the first seventy-two hours, Arrieta raved with delirium. He was unable to leave his bed for seven days, and when he finally could, he needed to use crutches to get around for another two weeks. Those of Arrieta's soldiers who witnessed these events say that never in their lives had they seen any man chew coca leaves, smoke tobacco, and drink *cañazo* like that old shaman had done during those first three nights of Arrieta's illness. Throughout this painful period, Yatiri never stopped reciting long prayers, chanting invocations, and screaming petitions. "I came to think that the young man was giving up the ghost," Yatiri said to his son Eleuterio, the majordomo of the Ninantaya Hacienda. "The second lieutenant's right thigh was swollen like the belly of a pregnant vicuña," stressed the old man as he gesticulated like a windmill.

* * *

Arrieta confided only in his orderly, Private Leoncio Quispe, of the adventures that he had with Yatiri during the time that he was bedridden. "He took me on a trip to

Umuchi," he told him one day. "Get serious, Pops," the soldier quickly responded, "You couldn't even walk while you were sick and Umuchi is ten leagues from here. Besides, why would the two of you go to Umuchi? You don't know anybody in that town, Pops." The young officer then said that Yatiri had asked him: "Would you like to go to Umuchi?" and that he had answered in the affirmative. "And then, in the blink of an eye, I realized that we were no longer in my room and the two of us were walking hand in hand through the streets of that town."

Arrieta had told Private Quispe that Yatiri had brought him there to show him Hilario's house, because that was the only place where he could kill that demon incarnate. "It's imperative that you kill him in that house. It's a matter of life and death for you," Yatiri had said.

* * *

Ever since Yatiri had spent those days of infirmity and convalescence so close to the second lieutenant, Hilario evolved into an ever more aggressive man. But at the same time, he was also warier of the presence and intentions of both the shaman and his protégé. On the one hand, he remorselessly killed other people's livestock, with his bare hands, while on the other hand he did the unspeakable to find out, through his spies, whatever possible information he could obtain about the activities of those two men.

* * *

During those nights of *cañazo*, coca leaves, prayers, and chants, when the young officer was ill, Yatiri revealed himself to be *Destiny's Overseer for that region*. The medicine man explained that even though Arrieta had come from Lima, fresh out of the military academy, his destiny was an intricate part of Ninantaya's reality and for that reason, it is important for the inhabitants of that hacienda. "You'll see this clearly once you find yourself obligated to participate in certain actions that are beyond your control," he said. He expanded upon this point by explaining that Hilario's intent was to lead Arrieta off his true path, to make him fail. "He's the son of the Devil, so try to take in the smell of sulfur when you're close to him. The stench is such that you'll be left without any doubts," said the old man. "Hilario wants to kill you. He has wanted to do this for many years now, ever since you were a child. I'm certain that you've seen him in your dreams many times before. That's how it happens, *taititaaa*!" he murmured next to Arrieta's ear with that toothless smile that was typical of him. "Sometimes destiny gets riled up, just like horses do, as you know, and we have to put it back on track. Destiny has a well-defined course which is calculated in such a way that it satisfies everyone on equal terms." During this conversation, Yatiri took advantage of tiny pauses between sentences to whisper ideas in the second lieutenant's ear. The young officer continually nodded, accepting what he was hearing and showing the shaman that he had understood perfectly what the old man was saying. Finally, one could hear Yatiri saying: "The only way to do it is with two shots in the head, in a cross formation" The young man couldn't believe what he had heard, but he repeated, word for word, the curious instructions he had received with great interest. Yatiri solemnly answered him: Yes, *taititaaa*, that's exactly right.

The people who attend the Saturday fair at Ninantaya's plaza converse amongst themselves throughout the day. In that market place, there isn't any news that the *colonos* don't comment on, mythologize, or refute. There, everyone talks about what people say someone who heard other people say told them. In the middle of all that chattering, they buy small amounts of quinoa seeds, maize kernels, grains of salt, and very tiny packages of sugar. One morning in the summer of sixty-five, during the Saturday fair, everyone excitedly commented on the discovery of Hilario's corpse by some door-to- door breakfast vendors. These people said that: a gendarme from Umuchi told one of the Bolivian drivers (given that he could not speak directly with anyone from Umuchi due to a gag order imposed by his boss, the first sergeant), that the deceased had his right femur broken in two parts, with one tip of the bone sticking out of the flesh. In addition, the departed had an entry wound, in the center of his forehead, caused by a .44 caliber bullet, which "exited through the occipital bone. You know the pointy one in the back of the head?"

The Bolivian driver also said that his friend, the policeman from Umuchi, reported that the dead body curiously had another entry wound, but of a smaller caliber, in the right temple, with a corresponding orifice on the other side of the head. The chauffer added that the trajectory of the two bullets was in the shape of a cross, which is the way in which one kills a devil incarnate. Officially, of course, the Civil Guard speculated that it was "a horrendous crime of revenge, or rivalry between bands of smugglers, or who knows, maybe even among drug traffickers." This last narrative, according to what the guardsman said, was the most plausible explanation, "because in these modern times one shouldn't believe in ghosts, or even demons."

Some of the people of Ninantaya believed that Yatiri eliminated Hilario. "He always spoke of Hilario as a demon incarnate," they said. Others defended the innocence of the poor old man, alleging that, according to the elders of that community, Yatiri had died in the year nineteen twelve. In fact, the person whom the villagers were accustomed to seeing and hearing as Yatiri was a mere reflection or a product of the collective memory of the community. This phenomenon was the result of the conjunction of their need to have a medicine man with the harsh reality of not having one. This group of inhabitants expressed the belief that the one who was responsible for the murder of Hilario was the famous Second Lieutenant Arrieta who had overseen the Ninantaya Hacienda two years ago. They spoke with an air of discontent about the authoritarian way in which the military officer had treated them. Yet, they never forgot the time when the Second Lieutenant became gravely ill because he had suffered an attack with a club that almost broke his right leg. From this event, they surmised that the second lieutenant had held Hilario responsible for this attack and had solemnly sworn that one day he would have his revenge.

Rumor has it that Eleuterio, Yatiri's son, could not affirm that his father had died in nineteen twelve, because Yatiri had dinner with him the night before, "Last night, *taititaaa*". Continuing his train of thought, Eleuterio affirmed that while he was enjoying his breakfast on the morning of the next day, "today in the morning, *papitooo*," he noticed that his father, the wise Yatiri, no longer sat down by the door of his house, where one could usually find him. For that reason, "it's difficult to know if my Pops is dead or alive, *papacitooo*." But speaking of death and murder, the majordomo said that his father could not have been the one responsible for such a horrendous crime, because he was a kind-hearted soul, incapable of harming any sulfur-stinking scoundrel, no matter how bad he may be.

Of course, the *colonos* of Ninantaya laughed every time they heard these stories. They knew that the Bolivians had killed Eleuterio on the day Second Lieutenant Arrieta and his soldiers tried to retake a little ravine, which the majordomo called "his" *quebradita*, from the hands of the damned Bolivians that robbed the Peruvians of it, back in nineteen fifty-six.

THE GUY WAS A QUEER

The Yearling[19], Cadet Aquilino Castillo, entered the central corridor of the campus dorms with a dazed look in his eyes. Instantly, the cadets loitering in the entryway of the hall began to guffaw and mock Castillo's haggard face: "where are you going, you-stupid parrot nose? Are you looking for your little friend? Why are you trembling, you queer? Man up, little faggot...!" Putting up with all his comrades' jeers, the harried Aquilino walked briskly, and with his head down, straight to the room of the only friend that he trusted. "If those brats had only been cognizant of what I was itching to report," thought Castillo, "then they would have curbed their euphoria in a fraction of a second."

As he walked along, the torrent of confusion that inundated the young man gradually turned into an unbearable vertigo. To avoid this uncomfortable malaise, the cadet raised his eyes and convinced himself that the capricious design of the peach flower granite floor, with its erratic black and white spots, was the sole cause of his dizziness. "I'm not dying!" he thought with clarity as he realized that his giddiness was only the product of an optical illusion. Upon arriving at the door-less entry of Cadet Arrieta's room, his anguish abated. At that moment, he recovered the composure that he so badly needed. "The guy

[19] Term used in US military academies for cadets in their second year; in Peru they are called, *Perro Viejo* (Old Dog).

was a queer!" he blurted out. And as he stood there with his free hand held high at the level of his abdomen, fingers spread out and trembling hysterically, he explained in a low tone of voice: "My friend, Captain Chumbeque, told me that, ten minutes ago."

* * *

Captain Chumbeque, the intelligence officer at the Paratroop School, was in the middle of a '*strictly* confidential' meeting with a group of concerned jump instructors. Although he patiently listened to the informal complaints of his colleagues, he was aware that he was not the proper authority to hear their grievances, veiled as they were. Nonetheless, the lieutenants and captains of the Paratroop School in attendance still felt the need to share their discomfort regarding certain actions on the part of a superior officer that they found to be incompatible with life on a military base. They said that they had observed something alarming in the behavior of Major Gonzalo Hermosa, the Chief Instructor. Due to the near unanimous opinion of all junior officers in attendance, Chumbeque saw clearly that the Chief Instructor was routinely abusing the power of his position.

The complainers added that Major Hermosa demeaned his subordinates with his ostentatious arrogance, which was apparently "inherited" from his wife's elevated social and economic status. "She's the daughter of General Del Toso, if you already didn't know," divulged 'Cockatoo' Diaz. "He thinks that his shit doesn't stink," said 'Parsley' González, contributing to the stack of accusations. "And I've heard him talk to himself in a loud voice in his room," mentioned 'Teetotum' Rodríguez, joining in on the assault. "He was talking about some guy, Oedipus, who must have been a pervert because the major ended up saying that he fucked his own mother." Finally, 'Crafty' Morales blasted, "He is a maniac; he thinks that he's the greatest thing since sunglasses. He preaches about honor and integrity as if he were God Himself."

* * *

Ever since Major Hermosa was a cadet at the military academy, his peers had accused him of being a brat. "He thinks he's an Adonis," Cadet Domínguez would say whenever he saw Hermosa walk past him. "That dumb ass thinks that he's either a prince, or the son of the President," the famous 'Crawfish' Carabelú muttered out of the side of his mouth when he saw Hermosa take command of the cadets' battalion. All his comrades agreed that ever since Hermosa first enrolled at the military academy, he had considered himself a cut above the rest.

Despite this consensus of implacable criticisms, his three roommates had a very different opinion about him. "He's the cleanest guy we know. He's more dedicated to his studies than anyone else, and is very respectful towards us," said Cadet 'Skull Face' Castro when his comrades-in-arms accosted him with questions, at some party or other on a Saturday night. "He solves all his problems using math, which he's thoroughly mastered," corroborated his roommate, 'Ginger' Murguía, between mouthfuls of *cebiche* paid for by an inquisitive cadet who knew of Murguia's weakness for raw fish.

The truth is that Hermosa had been a good cadet. He graduated with excellent grades and was always dressed in freshly pressed uniforms. Even so, in those days Hermosa had an idiosyncrasy that one could consider a defect: he always felt obligated to hit on women without caring whether they were beautiful or ugly. "Oh man! What a hot-looking chick! Did you see how she undressed me with her eyes?" Or whenever he cruised down Larco Avenue in his father's car, he'd say: "Hey, check out at that dumb broad! Her jaw drops at the very sight of me. She's practically drooling, but next to me, she's a piece of shit *chola*. I've had better." At times, his behavior was so egregious that he even surprised those who knew him very well. "What a tasty piece of ass she is! I'd eat that right now!" he'd say in a sexually excited tone of voice as he passed by.

Nonetheless, this outlandish conduct on his part was only witnessed by classmates at the time that Hermosa was a cadet. No such behavior could have been verified after he graduated the academy and became an officer.

* * *

The lieutenants and captains were irritated by the constant pressure to which the Chief Instructor subjected them. Consequently, the instructors began to meet secretly to exchange ideas and complaints, as well as some gossip, about the major. As time passed, the frequency of these meetings increased. The number of officers attending these gatherings gradually grew to the point that it was impossible for them to hold their sessions in just any dorm room. It would simply have been too risky, as well as uncomfortable, given that their conclaves were originally convoked for talking about their boss, the Chief Instructor. So, they opted to assemble on the soccer field instead, and agreed to congregate there three times a week, after 14:00 hours.

Dressed in their practice jerseys they played ball in a conspicuously languid manner and from time to time staged confrontations that were allegedly caused by ill-intentioned kicks to the legs. These simulated altercations allowed them to gather in one spot on the field around the supposedly injured party. That's where it all began.

One day, Lieutenant 'Cockatoo' Díaz reported, in an ambiguous tone, to having seen the Chief Instructor bring a military police sergeant to his living quarters. "There's nothing strange about that," answered a senior lieutenant, 'Screwball' Saavedra, who immediately added: "I frequently have my orderly come up to my room to shine my boots, belts and cross straps." And with his hands and arms spread out, he began to bob his head while saying: "Ah, ah, ah?" Lieutenant Díaz grabbed the two officers nearest him by the arms and said sotto voce: "That's the weird thing. Why would you bring a *black* MP Sergeant to your room?" All of them remained silent for a few seconds until "Screwball" Saavedra, staring fixedly at the grass, said that, according to his orderly, Major Hermosa was giving that black MP a calculus class in his room. Hearing this explanation, Captain Chumbeque retorted at the speed of an arrow: "He was giving his ass to that black MP, in his room, is what your orderly wanted to say." And everyone joined in with a silent laugh. They didn't want to raise any suspicions about the real reason for their meeting. "On the other hand," said the officer pretending to be a referee in the fake soccer game, "I can assure you that the major disappears after the second round of drinks in every luncheon that we've had at the Paratroop School." This last revelation produced an extraordinary effect on most of the conspirators accounted for. Their faces changed. Their eyes shined bright with a shameful mix of surprise and sarcasm. They all looked at each other and, at the same time, averted their eyes from each other's gazes.

In the patio in front of the restaurant of the Officer's Club, a mature officer, wearing riding breeches and boots, is seated at a wrought iron table with a younger officer with whom he is conversing. "Gonzalo, I've heard that you read disturbing books and that you do weird things in your base. Is this true?" asked General Del Toso of his son-in-law, Major Hermosa, between sips from his tall glass of whiskey. "I don't know what to think, son," the old officer confided to him in a paternal tone. After a brief pause and another swig of liquor, the general continued: "What could be so strange about reading? Could it be the subject matter of those books? What mess have you gotten yourself into, Gonzalito?" He bombarded him with questions that seemed more like thoughts expressed aloud and clinked his crystal glass against his son-in-law's, saying "*salud!*" Major Hermosa bit his lips, but maintained his composure. "Novels and one or two philosophy books," he answered. The general patted the major's shoulder and told him to act according to his station in life. "Think of your family. Think of me," he said, bidding him farewell and placing his empty glass on top of the table. He then smoothed out the wrinkles in his riding breeches, and marched off without looking at his son-in-law who remained seated, taking large swigs of his whisky and mineral water, wrestling with his adverse thoughts and the uneasiness with which the general, his father-in-law, had left him.

The afternoon meetings were becoming more spread out and the "soccer team" began to formulate their strategy: at every luncheon, or celebration of some historical event, they would designate at least two officers who were given the "mission" of deceiving all the other partygoers about their liquor intake. They needed to appear that they were imbibing, while they were remaining completely sober. The true objective of this "operation" was for these two officers never to lose sight of the major. These sober spies should follow him at a certain distance and carefully watch his movements. Thus, slowly but surely, the pieces of the puzzle came together and after two months of bird-dogging the major, the lookouts' report showed that the military police sergeant had made a considerable number of visits to the major's living quarters.

Later, one of the members of the "soccer team" informed the group that he had surprised the suspects in the guardhouse of the base, exchanging glances that could be considered inappropriate between men. "The looks they gave each other are the sensual kind I give to a chick that I fuck from time to time. She's a black girl that works in the Post Exchange," said Captain Olvera. "And may I add, that I would never think of looking at my wife in that way! It's the look that a whore gives a john. In short, I believe that they were jerking each other off with their eyes."

In the face of such "concrete evidence," all the "operatives" on the "soccer team" decided to go on the offensive, "which in any case is the best defense," said Captain Chumbeque. They agreed to move from mere observation to ambush. The motion was approved unanimously, but the team concurred on the need for a graphic piece of evidence, just before the ambush, to prevent their enterprise from going south. "Of course, said "Bandy Legs" Dávila, "this is a military operation. We should do some reconnaissance work to verify the enemy's position before attacking; just like Field Marshall Cáceres said, may he rest in peace, 'To hell with those sons of bitch Chileans!'"

"Okay, okay 'Bandy Legs.' Stop it! Don't go any further. We already know about your obsession with the war against Chile," said Captain Chumbeque. Dávila's feelings regarding the Chileans aside, the rest found 'Bandy Legs' observation to be coherent and they proceeded to draw up a blueprint of Hermosa's living quarters on base showing the key locations, in both the bedroom and the bathroom, where they planned to install hidden photographic cameras. They agreed that the 'mission' was to be carried out that weekend, in secret, and that all the participants in this 'operation' would be on the lookout so that all angles of approach would be covered. They decided that Sunday was to be D-day, and that 02:00 hours would be H-hour. The operation (which was deemed to be so highly classified that it had no name), would be coordinated and directed by Captain Epifanio Chumbeque Maravedí himself, who at the time was the S2[20] for the Paratroop School and had graduated from the army's military intelligence school. "I'll take charge of everything," said the captain. "I can borrow everything that we need from my alma mater." That weekend, after careful preparation, the cameras were installed and every phase of the project was executed with the utmost precision.

The following day, Monday, at 06:30 hours, after the frenzy of the weekend, Major Hermosa received an anonymous telephone call while he was tidying up the papers on his desk. Someone, who was passing himself off as a "colleague" of his, notified him, in a soft and delicate voice, that there was a possibility that certain members of the intelligence service may have been photographing the major's daily activities in both his bedroom and bathroom.

The major marched straight to his quarters like a bull bred for bullfighting. He ransacked his lodgings, turning over every piece of furniture and looking behind every picture frame and shelf, until he finally found the cameras. Hermosa was outraged. He shaved, put on his full-dress uniform, and placed two tables together covering them both

---

[20] The officer in charge of intelligence services in a military unit.

with a bed sheet. He got on top of this "burial mound," lay on his back and spent ten minutes smoothing out the wrinkles in his impeccable white coat and black trousers. Once his attire was perfect enough to pass muster, he placed his nine-millimeter pistol into his mouth, as if it were the nipple on a baby-bottle, and fired.

* * *

"Motherfucker!' muttered Cadet Arrieta through his teeth.

"What, you Arequipeño piece of shit? What do you think of that story? Talk, damn it! Cat got your tongue?" inquired Cadet Aquilino Castillo of his friend, Gerardo Arrieta, who simply stared at him, wide-eyed and open-mouthed.

"That's murder, you-dumbass!" clarified Cadet Arrieta. "They didn't take a single picture of Hermosa, did they? I know they couldn't have because the photographic cameras were only installed the day before. Do I have to spell it out for you? That was an assassination!" Cadet Arrieta repeated, shaking his head with disgust.

"Hold it right there, you-dipshit Arequipeño," said Aquilino. "Do you think that someone would kill himself over a sin that he didn't commit? Don't be so naive. There wasn't any need to take any pictures because the Chief Instructor *felt* guilty. He *was* guilty, and above all, *cholo*, can you imagine what that dumb shit could have been doing in his bedroom or bathroom that he felt compelled to take his own life? He probably thought that there were already pictures in the hands of all his colleagues and superiors, showing all those abominable things that he must have been doing with that black sergeant."

83

"Be that as it may, I still feel that there's something wrong; something just doesn't add up," said Cadet Arrieta. "Who in the intelligence service called Major Hermosa over the phone? How did they know what was going on with Hermosa?"

"No one, you dummy. Are you stupid or are you just pretending to be?" replied Cadet Aquilino Castillo.

"I don't pretend to be anything. I am who I am. I would never play dumb, you twisted Piurano," Arrieta said disparagingly.

"Yes, brother, I know that, and I also know that you are a great friend. Sorry for the jokes," said Aquilino. "The guy that made the call was my buddy, Captain Chumbeque, passing himself off as an anonymous faggot within the intelligence service. However, neither he nor any of the other members of the 'soccer team' ever thought that Hermosa would end up dead. Everyone simply believed that the major would be dishonorably discharged after the proper authorities in the army's G-2 headquarters received the pictures that the team was planning to take. What ended up happening to Hermosa was purely accidental. Chumbeque screwed the operation with that impromptu phone call.

"No one expected to cause that much damage. The 'soccer team' only wanted to punish a 'queer' that not only had crossed the line by wearing the sacred uniform of the Army, but, what's even worse, had done it while serving in the Paratroop School. Don't you think that what they did was right?"

DELIRIUM

"It's just the flu, Second Lieutenant; nothing to be afraid of Pops! Moreover, this is simply how this sickness comes: first, your temperature runs high, and then that fever opens your body up to all sorts of demons. Look, here comes the medic, Sergeant Valdés! He's going to cure you Pops," says Quispe while he holds the second lieutenant down by the shoulders, against his bed.

Night has fallen and the officer, bathed in sweat and curled up like a fetus, murmurs incoherent phrases about a white brick wall and a cherry tree. Outside the house, the rain drums on the corrugated sheet metal roof with the persistence of a mentally deranged man. The insanity of the racket produced by drops of water crashing against the crimped canopy, together with the whistling of the wind splitting in two as it hit the edge of the undulated zinc sheets, make their way through the inner ears of the unconscious officer. Suddenly, Arrieta shudders and stretches his extremities as if a lightning bolt had been running through his body from one end to the other.

"What's this pisspot doing on top of the nightstand!" shouts the medic upon entering Arrieta's bedroom. Private Quispe answers him that if he places it under the bed, as Valdés had ordered him, he can't comfortably approach the second lieutenant to dry his forehead because he'd turn over the chamber pot with the tip of his shoes. "Don't you see

85

that our shoes get under the bed when we approached?" he says to the sergeant, while he physically demonstrates what he had been saying. In that precise moment the medic, wishing to diagnose his patient, attempts to introduce a thermometer under the young officer's tongue. The second lieutenant opens his feverishly resplendent eyes and initiates a defensive maneuver by interposing his hands, fingers spread out as a sort of curtain, between his own face and the image of Valdés. Arrieta then paws the nightstand, with his right arm stretched out, in search of his pistol, and overturns the bedpan spilling urine all over Sergeant Valdés's legs. The medic jumps back amid a series of "fucks!" and "motherfuckers!" Quispe, Arrieta's orderly, defends his boss like a bird of prey. With his arms stretched out at either side of his body, fists closed; his chest puffed up, jaw thrust forward and lips like a beak, he raises his voice to say to the sergeant: "The second lieutenant is delirious! He doesn't know what he's doing; he needs your help Sarge!" The orderly then sits down at the edge of the metal bed where his boss is lying supine; takes the sick man's hand and he holds it down, while firmly pressing it with his own two hands, until he feels a cramp in his arms.

After immobilizing the young officer's feet with a cinch strapped over his legs and around the bed, Valdés dedicates himself to lighting some charcoal on a brazier. Once the fire's started, he places over it a clay pot full of fresh quinoa leaves, on which he sprinkles four dried chili peppers.

"Those are quinoa leaves, Sarge!" said Private Quispe, in between smiles, and raising his voice sarcastically.

"There aren't any eucalyptus trees for twenty leagues around, you-dumbass! Leaves are leaves and the chili peppers will replace the strong smell of the eucalyptus! We make do with what we have, right? Well, at least that's what *he* taught us," proclaims Valdés.

The second lieutenant, between coughs and chokes due to the spicy smoke, continues to babble phrases having to do with a white brick wall; plants; and dogs that died of asphyxia. Meanwhile, he finds himself immobile because his hands are held down by his orderly, and his shoulders are pinned to his mattress by the medic. So Arrieta surrenders and goes back to Morpheus' prison house.... But in his delirious state he keeps talking in a loud voice.

* * *

"Standing in front of the white brick wall, under the cherry tree, I feel as if a profound sorrow has taken me by surprise," thinks a juvenile Arrieta, astonished by the place in which he finds himself. The second lieutenant contemplates his delirious image and he admires the enraptured attitude that his figure exhibits as it declaims, with precision and patience, a text that is not his own, but which still sounds familiar. He comes to realize that he is dreaming due to the musical tone of his discourse, full of metaphors that are foreign to his day-to-day language. He knows that it's a dream, but he resigns himself to live through it because he is conscious that dreams have a life of their own and that he can't get out of them. Consequently, he gives in, pays attention, and listens to what his nightmare forces him to say:

"Sorrow arrives, in silence, and it adheres to my skin like a soaked bed sheet. The knot that I had in my throat has violently come undone, inundating my eyes with a bitter liquid. Where are you, mother, that you don't speak to me as you did before? How is it that you leave me alone in this empty house, in the middle of an abandoned garden, facing this white brick wall that looks me in the eyes with desolation and bewilderment? I've strolled through your garden, among the rocoto pepper bushes; a white peach tree; various broom bushes; and a slipper gourd plant, only to find no response. I've contemplated, without overcoming my doubts, your geraniums, lilacs, the prolific asparagus, and lilies clustered against the wall. I've seen, with much pain, the destruction and the abandonment that have invaded our garden. The yellowish leaves of the news daily El Pueblo, here and there, attached, by the wind, to the contours of scattered rocks. The rusted tin cans, full of dry soil, now the living quarters of black witch moths and slimy snails, where once were found your clay pots plagued with multicolored flowers; the arid soil, in every place, splashed with weeds where once flourished light and the aroma of rosemary and lemongrass. I've observed spiders spinning their webs over ticks that drag themselves between the orifices on the volcanic bricks of our garden's white wall, struggling to save their minuscule lives. The pestilent skeleton of a bitch, under the pepper tree, loyal guardian of the tomb where her pups rest, suffocated by papa many times over, inside a burlap sack. Absent mother, you've left me like a hatchling outside of the nest; I need your presence in this foggy path of mine. I've just turned twenty-three; I have my doubts and a few well-founded suspicions, but I know where I'm going. I don't demand much, mama, I only need, by my side, your verbal complicity; someone who will love me and will not hesitate to sink when I sink; who authorizes my failure and who has the tendency to celebrate second attempts. I must travel to the heart of my being until I find that which asphyxiates me. Come here, mama, sit at the edge of my madness and, with your skinny hand, run your fingers through the docile hairs on my head. Help me to remember!" says Arrieta aloud, in his sleep, and continues to follow the script written by his nightmare.

"Who are you Isabel?" asks the young Arrieta.

"I'm your mother. What a presumptuous little snotnose!"

"If so, then who's Mama Gertrudis?"

"Your aunt, my beloved sister."

"I think, at times, that she is my mama."

"She raised you for only two and a half years. I'm your *real* mother!"

"Did Mama Gertrudis breastfeed me, Mama Isabel?"

"She couldn't have! She is an *unmarried* woman. She doesn't have breast milk. Unmarried women's breasts are just for *show!*"

"Liberata says..."

"Don't even mention *her!* She's just an old gossip, who's clumsy and stupid. Her head is full of cobwebs. She doesn't know the truth. Do you hear me? Don't you even mention her again; *I'm* your mama. You came out of *my* womb, and *nobody* can deny it."

"And how come I don't have a grandfather, Mama Isabel?"

"It's because he's dead."

"And what did he die of?"

"Shame; he died of shame."

"What was he ashamed of, mommy?"

"He was an important notary in Arequipa when his son, the oldest, abusing his good faith and paternal love, did I don't know what kind of shenanigans with some dossiers and papa could no longer resist that ignominy. Your poor grandfather died of shame and let that be very clear to you."

"Ah! Just like Liberata told me. The old maid related to me that, *'there was an unexpected noise coming out of the bathroom. It sounded very loud when your grandpa fell. Nobody dared go through that door. The smell of blood let us know that he was dead. And when they found this out, the women of the house commenced their crying, their complaints, and their recriminations. They pulled their hair out and tore their garments until the arrival of your uncle whose name is Gerardo, just as your grandfather's name is Gerardo, and you too are named Gerardo. Moreover, it was he, your uncle Gerardo, who was the only one brave enough to enter the bathroom, while in the meantime your aunts and your mommy too, and the maidservants also, shouted and scratched the hard, plaster walls until they broke their fingernails and stained the paint with streaks of their own blood. And then your grandmother, dear boy, the sainted woman started to faint in the middle of the room and we were losing her...little by little, we were losing her; and I, the old Liberata, had to use some ammonia to make her come back.'*

"And just as I finish telling this story, my mama Isabel questions me again; she asks what else the old busybody told me. I tell her everything. I tell her that Liberata also said to me, '*that your Uncle Gerardo came out of the bathroom stained red like our homeland's flag. That drenched in blood, he dragged your grandfather, who weighed a lot, dear boy, up to the bed where he laid him down and fixed up his face, by picking up pieces of his head from the bathroom floor, and patching up his skull until it looked the same as when he was alive.*'"

"Shame explodes heads, mama! That's why mine will also blow up and spread all over the room when I die, dearest mommy," says the young Arrieta in a loud voice, because he can't contain himself any longer.

"And my grandmother, mommy, where is she? Did she also die of shame, mommy?"

"No, she died of sorrow. It was impossible for her to live with the death of her beloved husband and three months after papa passed away, she left forever, overwhelmed by the anguish of not being able to see him. And when she died, to everyone's disgrace, it happened just right after she gave birth to my sister, Josefa, the youngest."

"And so, then, it won't be very long before I die too, mama."

"Why do you say that, my beloved son?"

90

"Because I feel shame and am tormented by sorrow, mama. There is something here inside my stomach and I can't tell what it is; and yet I understand that it turns about like a spinning top and moves under my ribs like the little dogs inside the burlap sack every time that papa would bury them in the garden."

"Go on dummy, those things are for grownups. They were killed by the kind of shame and sorrow that only affects adults, because these emotions are so intense in nature that they can be unbearable and in some cases even fatal. It's almost ten AM; it's time for your mid-morning snack. Eat your salad, then go out and play. Go to the garden, Gerardito; play with the dog; eat some cherries; arrange a snail race!"

*   *   *

"Don't pull those covers off, Second Lieutenant! Open your mouth and drink this hot mate de coca; mate with Pisco; it's good for the flu!" says Quispe, while the medic applies a wet rag, as a kind of poultice, on the feverish forehead of the sick, young man.

"The Devil!" says the second lieutenant shouting and attempting to lift his torso, only later to fall back to sleep under the pressure of his two caretakers holding him down.

Hours later, Arrieta renews his struggle and demands that he be brought his riding boots, his work uniform, and his arms; "I need to go to the border!" he shouts. "Hilario is approaching from the south to collect our souls; there is no time to lose!" In the altercation that ensues, both the 'patient' and his two 'doctors' perspire profusely, but after a hard-fought battle the young officer finds himself the victor when his two soldiers, their strength having been exhausted, cease to resist. The febrile officer, pistol in hand, stands on his bed. His sense of balance is precarious due to the sunken form of the spring mattress base and the thin metal bands that constitute its lean structure. Valdés, the medic, shouts at him, bitterly, "Sir, the mattress is caving in! You're going to fall down and crack your head open!" But the second lieutenant doesn't pay any attention to any mere mortal and continues with his own routine. And so, when Arrieta, drooling a brown foam and challenging Satan himself, fires his first shot at the ceiling, the medic Valdés hits him on the back of the head with the canteen full of the mate de coca that he had been giving the sick young man, by the spoonful, since the day before. The young officer, under the impact, collapses in the arms of Quispe, who had been standing in front of his boss for as long as he and Valdés had been pleading with him.

"What did you do to him, Sarge? He's pissed himself with that blow you gave him to the head!" says Quispe while he straightens out the blankets and prolifically covers the body of the second lieutenant who once more closes his eyes and rests with a contorted face.

*   *   *

And the yellow, curly haired child burst into the living room, like a waterspout, to say that something terrible had just happened to him. His mother contemplated him while she swallowed a sigh and asked him if it was the Devil again. The young sapling, straightening his curls with both hands, nodded ostensibly with his head and told her that "yes, mama, it had been the Devil" who, as usual, came for him. That the red-faced one chased after him in a pampa, and that he, desperate and in a hurry, ran without being able to make any headway. That his feet, were moving like the wheels on a steam locomotive, "and just as fast, mama, but because they never touched the ground, I never advanced, mother dearest. While on the other hand, the horned one could close in on me with an evil visage and fiery eyes, and managed to bruise my little back with a red-hot lance, mommy dearest!" And continuing, with a voice that sounded dramatically like that of an adult, he implored her to save him, to take this load off his shoulders; that he didn't want to go on living. The contrite mother demanded him, "for God's sake! Take that bitter sorrow out of your heart and tell me what is tormenting you, my little angel?" The boy, babbling, answered her that, "it's the Devil, mommy...who is Hilario, Isabel?"

Isabel's face turned pale. She almost choked. Visibly perturbed, she fanned her face with both hands. She dried the sweat on her forehead and her nose with a small pink handkerchief. She coughed and her shortness of breath evinced her anguish; with a lost look in her eyes, and full of rage, she told him: "He was the *servant* whom we dismissed just weeks ago." Later, with an infinite amount of curiosity, she asked him if that young Aimara had done something bad to him. The boy answered her that, "I don't remember anything, mommy." He said something that she understood as: "Only his name haunts me and brings the Devil with it, but nothing of his face, much less of his appearance, size, or tone of voice."

* * *

Given the expression of tranquility on the second lieutenant's face during those last ten minutes, the two men by his side decided to set him upright on his bed; however, they remained alert to any indication of craziness on the part of the officer, despite the fatigue that ailed them both. Gerardo Arrieta opened his eyes and said, without a vestige of any bad intention on his part: "I'm going to puke." He then proceeded to return, from his stomach, a torrent of vomit that impregnated the room with the nauseating smell of sour food. After this, the second lieutenant went back to resting with his eyes half-closed, while Quispe and Valdés, hands, and knees on the ground, cleaned up what had just been spilled, in between mordant comments on the orderly's part. Valdés shouted at Quispe that this was not a game, and that he should stop clowning around, to which the private, between forced laughs, responded that: "Well, at some point we have to laugh, Sarge. We can't always be so serious all the time like the second lieutenant..."

*　*　*

Liberata, the old maidservant, says:

"Have more respect for the wall, you ill-mannered child, or you won't be able to sleep tonight. I'm warning you; in *that* wall is your grandfather Gerardo," she recites half-closing her eyes, until she makes them like the slot on a piggy bank, scrunching up her aquiline nose, stiffening her bulbous cheek bones and making a mess of the grizzled hair on her head through which her voice becomes intermeshed.

"I tell Liberata that I don't believe her. I reiterate, as I tense up the muscles on my face, that nobody lives in *that* wall, or in that *other* wall, or in the *ceiling*, or in the *piano*, as you say, Liberata. I emit an opinion and tell her that I believe that she is either drunk or crazy, or that she is like a child, being so short, because she doesn't know that the dead gallop throughout the universe in absolute freedom. I confess to her that certain nights, the Devil chases after me and that when he does, he floats over the pampa, rolls over the rivers and slides along, riding on the waves of the sea. Liberata shoots me a sidelong glance and says to me that I'm an irreverent snotnose. She keeps quiet for a while, and then she says to me, as she squints, that there is something that I have to respect, that: 'there are *errant* souls and there are *condemned* souls. Errant souls can wander about freely. But the other ones, oh! Abandoned in this world and circumscribed by a specific place they are, until some particular sin that they've committed, which is awaiting reparations, has finally been clarified.' Later she states that what she will proceed to say is definitive: 'In *that* wall, close to the bathroom, is your grandfather Gerardo. In the old *piano*, resides Mamita Rosita, your great-grandmother.' What's more, the old woman says that, 'the departed don't have bodies like ours; they only have height and width; they don't have *any* thickness left.' And since I'm not able to understand all that well what she means to say, she reaffirms that 'they're photographs with a transparent background. That's all, you-snot-nosed little shit! They're just an *image*,' she clarifies; 'but they have *feelings*; they *suffer* with all that they see,' she says to me with delirious eyes. That '*this* is their Purgatory,' the old Liberata tells me, and she continues talking in Aimara, spitting various times, foamy saliva, and crossing herself every now and then. After this, she breathes sonorously, three consecutive times and tells me, 'And I, so you can understand very well, am neither a girl, nor a *midget*, and even though you may not believe it, I'm nothing more than a woman *shrunken* by old age. Your day will come. You'll see! You *too* will shrink!'"

"I see my mother again and I ask her why I can't play with Jorge and Alberto today? She, raising her body from the bench where she had been sitting, begins a long and well-known response. She says that Jorge is the son of the tailor and Alberto that of the shoemaker. That they are both *cholitos* and that I am a child of means. 'We may not have money, now, yet you should know that we are very *decent* people,' she says as if reciting from a pedestal. Later she adds that my grandfather owned almost the entire city and was a well-respected *señor*. That many people came to the house for lunch and for dinner, and that they would render him homage and call him *caballero* Gerardo. That his Mama Julia possessed a vineyard, inherited from her parents, 'the Rivera family, who were *very* much a family of means!' What's more, as she had already explained to me, on repeated occasions, with the tragic loss of her papa it was discovered that he had given away, without the family's knowledge, the better part of his properties. After saying this last bit, she became nervous and almost shouted: 'Sonny, your grandfather was a good man and I don't want you to pass judgment on his gifts and his charities. It's enough for you to know that we are *decent* people and that's the reason you can't hang around with just any *cholito*.' Upon reaching this point in her discourse, I intervened by contributing information that she was unable to digest. I told her that Mama Gertrudis had authorized me to play with whomever I so desired; and that she says yes to me, every time; and more importantly, mama, she always, always, tells me the truth.

"Isabel got upset. She asked me to listen to her from here to eternity: '*I* am your mother.' Then she added that I always put her nerves on edge; that her neuralgia destroyed the left side of her face. Finally, she insisted, 'Lord Jesus, I don't know what I'm going to do with you! You make me cry. You drive me insane!'

"After this, mommy puffed up and, with a shrill voice, said to me, 'No, no, no; you can't play with the *cholos*. Do *you* understand me?'

"I felt sad and asked her, that if that's the case, then who am I going to play with, mama? There aren't any *decent* people around here, mommy dearest. To the right, there's Jorge, the son of the tailor; and further up is Alberto, son of the shoemaker; and on the corner lives General Ramírez, who *doesn't* have any offspring. And to the left, mommy, the house of Mama Gertrudis, your beloved sister; after which comes the dwelling of Emilito, your younger brother; and in continuation Torres Ramírez, the 'Painter' who *never* opens his door. Further on one finds the apartments of Mama Belita, Aunt Josefa and Aunt Sofía, who are no longer little girls, *mom*; and beyond them only *cholitos*, the newspaper boys who sell the dailies in the early morning. Then you have Ugarte the carpenter, who is a fanatical *Aprista*[21]; and lastly the infamous 'Earless Cat[22]' who lives one month in his house and the other eleven that are left in the Siglo Veinte penitentiary...With *whom*, then, will I be able to play with, mother dearest?"

* * *

"That's the way we like it, second lieutenant; stay nice and quiet. It's what's best for you. If you behave well, we'll loosen your legs. Just like that. Nice and quiet is how we like it," say Valdés and Quispe, one sentence apiece, while they breathe deeply, dry their hands on their pant legs, and both forcefully scratch their scalps. Then, after looking each other in the eye for an instant, as if seeking to buttress their 'medicinal' efforts thus far, the two men drink large sips of mate de coca from the canteen until the receptacle, having been turned upside down, only let fall a couple of drops. Meanwhile, the officer lies sound asleep with a smile beginning to form on his lips.

A half hour later, the 'patient' rejoins the group: "I want to take a shit," he says with a raspy voice; he clears his throat and spits residual pieces of food without paying

---

[21] A member of the Peruvian political party APRA, which stands for Alianza Popular Revolucionaria Americana, or American Popular Revolutionary Alliance.

[22] His nickname was in fact "Gato Ccoro," which is a combination of Spanish and Quechua, and it meant "a cat with very short, or no ears."

attention as to where they may fall. His men observe him, they exchange glances and shrug their shoulders; they help him to lower his feet and stand up completely. Afterwards, they cover him with a blanket; put on his shoes, without tying them; don their rain ponchos, and drag him outside to take him to the latrine. There they sit him down and turn their faces away with their noses tilted up towards the cold wind and the rain. Quispe shouts at Valdés, over the noise of the storm, that the second lieutenant is rotting, that his crap smells like a dead donkey. Valdés answers him that: "He's just now beginning to expel all the evil that he had within him; first, with the vomit, and *now* with this foul-smelling shit." After the second lieutenant has concluded that natural function of the body, the soldiers take him back to his bed where he closes his eyes and, breathing agitatedly, trembles again to go once more back to sleep.

"Do you think, Sarge, that he's going to keep on sleeping, or is he going to be a bother again?" Quispe asks, as he places anew the moist rags that cover the forehead and ears of the second lieutenant making the young man look like a newly consecrated nun.

"Be careful, you dumb *cholo*; you have to rinse those rags! Don't let *any* water get into his ears!" Sergeant Valdés shouts in a hushed tone of voice, as he mimics the act of extracting water from a wet fabric by wringing it tightly with his hands. The officer on the bed gently brushes his right ear with his fingertips, as if he were scaring off insects surprised in the act of repeatedly intending to penetrate his ear canal. "Wipe those drops of water he has in the vestibule of his outer ear," says Valdés to Private Quispe. To which the orderly responds between guffaws, "They look like glass earrings, don't they?"

The three of them were awakened by an abrupt silence that flooded the house when the wind and the rain had ceased. The 'patient' said: "I can't breathe through my nose," and his whole body began to tremble. The medic suggested to him, "Well then just breathe through your mouth, second lieutenant;" and the sick young man retorted that his throat was burning up, that he lacked the strength, and that he felt like this was the end of the line for him. The two men looked at him and, with their heads lowered, said in a chorus, "Fuck, there's nothing left for us to do but just pray: Our Father..." they began in a loud voice, kept going until they finished, and later began to once more pray, and pray, and pray.

* * *

"At the La Salle parochial school, things didn't go all that bad. Soon enough, there arrived the preparatory talks for the first communion. In them, we discussed more vehemently about what could happen if we took a bite of the sacred host, and about the intensity of the experience of being one with God, at least for an instant. In those days, I felt content and began not only to experience the adventure of confronting the realities of those people surrounding me, but also that of defining my own criteria about life. Everything led me by the hand, without any pitfalls, up to the Holy Eucharist, however I still swore that something bad existed within my body; something that was unknown to me, but which at the same time I suspected was like a dead puppy crouching at the top of my stomach.

"I soon summoned enough courage and went to the priest that had been assigned to hear my confession and told him that I had a doubt. 'What is it about, my son?' he asked me, upon sitting down and putting his over-sized right hand over my head. I confessed that I was sure I had a dead puppy, here, inside my stomach. That the little animal was curled up like a ball, with its mouth open, like this, Father, (I said scrunching my nose and baring my teeth like a mad wolf) to look even more ferocious upon making a ridiculous expression with its snout, Father. He answered me, 'that's impossible, my child,' and that I should stop thinking about that nonsense. 'Or do you want to go to the doctor?!' he shouted, as he gasped for air. In such a difficult situation as this, I argued as well as I could, and said no; please, not the doctor, Father. I told the rotund priest that what I wanted to ask him was: what will happen if when I take Holy Communion and the Sacred Host enters into my stomach; let's say; just in case; as a supposition, that the puppy should happen to be there? And the priest shouted, 'And here we go again!' After wheezing a bit, Father José Luís continued: 'I'm going to send a note to your parents, and see if they will take you to the doctor and free us of any doubts, once and for all,' and he said this with a thunderous voice and a face as red as the Devil's."

* * *

"He already slept a good while without any bother," said Sergeant Valdés, with the authority of a primary care physician. He immediately added, "How about I go lie down in your bed, Leoncio, while you rest here on these bags of clothing, so we both can get some sleep as well?" Quispe answered, "Agreed. I'll call you if anything strange happens, Sarge." Yet, when the medic attempted to retire, he kicked, without realizing it, a piece of wood that stuck out of a group of objects that had accumulated at one end of the room. Instantly, a whole pile of military equipment (including the second lieutenant's steel helmet, various ammunition cartridges, and a mess kit), were scattered about, hitting the cement floor with a sound reminiscent of machine gun fire. History always feels the need to repeat itself, and no matter how miniscule the event may be, it is no less exempt from this monotonous addiction. And so, it was in this manner that the second lieutenant, once more,

100

moved his arms about, like out-of-control windmill blades. As he initiated a defensive maneuver, with no aim in mind, the two men were forced to stifle him with a great deal of effort and many a spoonful of mate de coca crammed down the young officer's throat. "You have to duck, Second Lieutenant; you're going to hit your head against the ceiling," his men shouted at him, upon subduing him, "you have to stretch yourself out on the bed, second lieutenant," they said repeatedly upon trying to make him return to a horizontal position.

* * *

"'You have to walk on all fours, Gerardito, as if you were crawling. Duck down, lower your head, and stretch out on the carpet. If you want to play, do it under the table; can't you tell that they can kill you? There's a revolution outside! It's the stray bullets that are the most dangerous!' preached Mama Gertrudis. 'These barbaric soldiers are shooting at everything that moves. Things are terrible downtown. Juanito Quezada told me that they're killing the people. He went to City Hall to pay his water bill when the shooting started no more than half an hour ago. Do you hear the cathedral bells, Gerardito? They're sounding the clarion call. Oh, my God! How the people are running through the streets! Where are those fools going? They'll kill them all. Jesus, how could this be happening?! This is nineteen fifty; we're living in a civilized, modern city! Don't you move, sweetie!' Mama Gertrudis reiterated upon making me crawl as if I were a baby who was still being breastfed. I told her that I wanted to go and see what was happening downtown, and she, with a dour look on her face, shouted at me that, 'You should stay right where you are. You're just a nine-year-old turd! It cost me a great deal just to keep you alive,'

Mama Gertrudis paused for a while, and then she added, 'Up until now that is to say...'

"I had to resign myself. She was much bigger than I was. Okay, mama, I told her. I heard you. I'll stay right here, under the table, and as I said this, I proceeded to lay down on the smelly carpet on which everyone treads, day in and day out."

* * *

As he heads out to urinate, Sergeant Valdés stops at the foot of the bed of the officer and inquires of Quispe, "How's the 'patient'?" "He's getting calmer and calmer every time, Sarge," answers the orderly. He then informs the medic that the second lieutenant, "still cringes every now and then, and that when he grinds his teeth, his eyes squirm under his eyelids as if they were wind-up toys, Sarge."

The medic explains to him, in an authoritative tone, that, "it must be the nightmares, Leoncio;" he says that nightmares sent by the Devil usually move one's eyes as Quispe describes, and he quickly continues to make his way to the latrine. The orderly then turns to look at the second lieutenant sprawled on the bed. As he smooths out the blanket and pulls the bed sheet up to the patient's chin, Quispe, an optimist by nature, shouts that, "Despite everything, my pop's face seems to be calmer than before, isn't that right, Sarge?" Valdés retraces his steps and goes back into the room to verify what Quispe had told him. He answers, "It certainly looks like it, Leoncio." He adds, "I believe the patient's going to recuperate, but for now the fucker's going to feel a little weak before his health really begins to improve." Valdés then gave the reason for his diagnosis: "It's been two long days now, Quispecito, in which the second lieutenant has been spewing out a torrent of crazy words. Now I want to hear him talk like a Christian who is in his right mind, for God's sake. Let me go, Leoncio; I think I've started to piss myself, you moron! And if I wet my pants, you're the only one responsible you talking-machine."

* * *

"Smelling ripe cherries and staining my ass chalk white, as I sit on top of this brick wall, I can tell you mother dearest, that I was only happy when I was by the sea, in Ocoña. Here, in this arduous, so-called white land, I've had intensely glorious moments; but I've only been happy, I mean really happy, at the beach. There, when I'm completely alone, I don't sense any shame at all. This is the only time when I really feel like myself in the entirety of my being, because as I stand there with my bare feet on that wet sand, scratching my naked belly as I face those capricious blue waves, I find true peace. In the end, mother dearest, I still wake up at night, covered in sweat, with the sensation that I have something rolled up inside my belly, just below my sternum. That is why I have come to put my bones in front of this dirty, white brick wall to see if she, unlike everyone else, is capable of telling me what the hell I'm looking for..."

* * *

"You were unconscious for three days, Second Lieutenant. You spit on us, you hit us, and you also covered us with insults and curse words," Quispe tells his convalescing boss, as he puts on an expression of false grief. The young officer replies that he doesn't remember anything; that he's sorry; that he's ashamed, and that he extends his thanks to all those who watched over him during his illness. "I need only a couple of days to recover my strength!" he tells them with a borrowed smile, and a gaunt expression, while he lies stretched out over his bed without even attempting to sit up or prop himself up on his elbows. "We are all feeling weak, Second Lieutenant," the medic informs him with his pale, lean face, and his cold bluish-purple ears; "we need meat, beans, real food, Sir!" Valdés says finally. "Shall we kill a little lamb, Second Lieutenant?" says the other sergeant, whose last name is Mayu, intervening in the conversation. "How about just a tiny one, Sir?" adds Corporal Huallpa, almost imploring. But the officer doesn't concede. He explains that if it is true that they have gone for three months without receiving any food supplies from the main operating base in Otabala, he maintains his faith in the army. He wants to be very clear about this: he will not allow anybody to think that their superior officers are pocketing those supplies for themselves. It is just a question of days. Their food supplies *must* arrive.

"Regarding the sheep, I have to inform you that they are an asset of the hacienda. If any one of those sheep goes missing, I will have to explain the reason for the disappearance of said animal. In the worst-case scenario, I could be sued by the regional high command. Just give me two days to get back my strength and we'll go hunt vicuñas to eat some meat, I promise!" says the second lieutenant in a conciliatory tone. Yet, one can tell by his voice that the officer is tired, nauseated, and breathing with difficulty. And so, Valdés, the medic, with all the authority of a 'physician,' dismisses the rest of the troop and prescribes for his patient some R&R and chicken soup, that they can prepare with the hen that the village telegrapher had recently brought, as a gesture of 'goodwill,' to aid in the officer's speedy recovery. Afterwards, when they are alone, Valdés turns to look for Quispe and tells him in a subdued tone of voice, "*Two* days? Bullshit! He's going to need at *least* one more week."

THE GHOST

I'm walking to my Uncle Tomás' house. He sent for me. What for? I don't know. I don't think that I did anything out of the ordinary. Or perhaps he already knows about the few guns that I sometimes bring with me from La Paz. I am afraid that my uncle will get mad at me, like he did with my younger brother, Germancito. My little brother had abandoned his post after he had been given specific orders to take care of a coffee shipment that was left stuck in the middle of the pampa when our truck broke down. Who knows how my uncle will react when he sees me? In any case, I'll ask for his forgiveness.

* * *

People say that Germán died from a gunshot to the forehead. I couldn't see my little brother before he was buried, so I can't say if what they mumble about how he died is true or not. The rumor floating around is that two days after that same coffee shipment was confiscated by the second lieutenant in charge of the Ninantaya Hacienda, my Uncle Tomás shot Germán when he was on his knees, begging to be forgiven for his disobedience on that 'coffee job.' This transgression on the part of my brother occurred

106

on the night that we were coming from Puerto Acosta, in Bolivia, with a truck full of coffee beans. That was the load that my uncle had authorized us to transport, but Germán insisted on bringing a few firearms and two bags of cocaine ready to be snorted. When we crossed the border, at nightfall, the truck's engine died on us. I left Germancito in charge of the shipment, buried the guns and the coke, and trotted to my Uncle Tomás' house. He received me in an apparently good mood. I told him that the truck couldn't go a step further and that it was stranded in the middle of the pampa, within the confines of the Ninantaya Hacienda. He then gave instructions for his chauffer to bring the truck that he kept parked in his backyard and shouted at the top of his lungs to wake up two *cholos* who were sleeping in his kitchen. Uncle Tomás explained to them that they were to follow my orders for as long as it took to solve the problem regarding the coffee shipment. He said that it was imperative that we get that truck out of the Hacienda before sunrise. My uncle yelled at us that we needed to act as fast as possible to avoid any intervention on the part of that army officer who lives on the Hacienda. "That pain-in-the-ass likes to wake up at 6 AM every day so he can roam around that area in search of any little thing that he can blame on me and mine," my uncle said to me.

As I approach my uncle's house, the smell of vinegar and pork comes out to greet me. "Adobo," I say to myself. "They certainly must have eaten adobo for lunch," I reason, but then I take a peek through the window and see Tarzan, my Aunt Angelina's German shepherd lying under the dining room table. From what I can tell, Tarzan appears to be gnawing on a raw pig's leg with a bluish hue. Could that almost rotten meat be the reason I'm sensing the smell of

Adobo? My brother Hilario told me that, on one occasion, our uncle ordered Tarzan to attack a custom agent and the fucking dog mauled that *cholo* to death. "That dog's dangerous; he likes the taste of raw meat." I ponder, but I keep this to myself.

I don't think that my uncle is here. Why would he have ordered me to come at four o'clock in the afternoon if he wouldn't be here? We work for him without any complaints at all. It´s true that he pays us, but not much. I mean with all the kinds of "businesses" that he handles, he could afford to pay more. Then again, he's always complaining that there is never enough money; that he has too many "payments" to make to keep his "businesses" afloat. Of course, he's our uncle and, being the kind of family that we are, we got to assist him in any way that we can.

Where could this fucker be? This is really beginning to bother me. Come to think of it, I believe that I could go into business for myself and make more money that way. Now...I'm not talking about putting my uncle out of business. It's just that I believe that with all the contraband that passes through here, there's plenty of work for all of us. No, he wouldn't dream of giving us that much free rein. I know of several who tried to go off on their own, but, when my uncle found out, we never saw or heard from them again. If I try to do the same, I'm positive that he would whack me himself. My uncle only kills blood relations. As for the rest, he uses an enforcer, and my little brother Germán always lent himself to this task. In my family, we all like to kill, a little; but Germán loved it even more. In fact, whenever there is a fair in Ninantaya, the people who congregate in the plaza like to gossip that even after Germán's death, my uncle still likes to use my younger brother's services. It's that Germancito was so keen on taking the life of other Christians. People say that even now, whenever Uncle Tomás needs him, my little brother Germán, despite being six feet under, will instantly appear at my uncle's house without being formally summoned by him. On these occasions, it is said that my uncle would usually open his front door and find Germancito sitting on his doorstep, awaiting his instructions. Well... at least that's what they say.

And now, what could I do if Uncle Tomás wants to kill me...? Shall I ask him to forgive me? Or maybe what I gotta do is jump the gun and whack him first, without any questions...without letting him say a word... And what if he's watching me right now? How do I know for sure? Perhaps that's why they call him the Ghost. But I could wait for him with a gat in my hand and inside my jacket pocket (as people say that my Uncle Tomás sometimes does), ready to shoot him without ever having to extract my pistol. In the end, this coat is already worn out and I don't think that a bullet hole will diminish its value.

If only my brother Hilario were here with me, right now. I think that my uncle has a certain amount of respect for him. It's because Hilario is courageous. He's the freest man that I've ever known. He kills animals with his bare hands. I've seen him put his arm, up to his elbow, into the belly of a live vicuña. When he took his arm out of that steaming cavity, he had the little animal's heart in his hand. Hilario loves me very much. That time, he ate half of the vicuña's heart and gave me the other half to eat. The two of us ate with delight. Afterwards, our lips were left covered with still-lukewarm blood. Hilario dislikes that second lieutenant who is currently in charge of the Ninantaya Hacienda. The night I placed Germancito in charge of the coffee shipment while I went to notify my Uncle Tomás about what happened to us, the young army officer had gone to the pampa and located our truck. Since Germancito was not there, that son-of-a-bitch grunt, with the help of his soldiers, was able to unload the fifty kilo bags of coffee, all two hundred of them, and open every goddamn coffee bean, in search of contraband. My brother Hilario wants to kill that 'little officer'; but my uncle says 'no,' because there is something strange going on between that rascal and the hacienda's Yatiri. He says that he doesn't want to deal with any more complications than the ones that his work already gives him.

Fuck! Here comes my uncle! My palms are already beginning to sweat and I feel a strange icy sensation spreading from my balls to my asshole! Uncle Tomás approaches me and, as is his custom, he puts his hand on the back of my neck to make me walk. I feel a grave sorrow hanging over my nape. Dryness invades my entire mouth. He says: "Hello, nephew. We have to have a talk," but he doesn't say anything more. I suddenly feel like I need to take a piss. He moves about and performs mundane tasks, but all the while doesn't say a word. Could it be because his mom, Aunty Evangelina, is already in bed and sleeping? Or it could it be for another reason... but he doesn't say anything to me and I begin to tighten my belt because my pants are feeling a little loose, as if they suddenly wanted to collapse on the floor.

My uncle's dwelling is made of stones and mud. We make our way through the penumbra of the rooms and cross the living room, the dining room, and various bedrooms. I ask him permission to go to the bathroom, and in between smiles, he mumbles that I can use it. After peeing, I come out and he grabs my neck again. We go to the kitchen and from there I can see the back of the house, a large dirt yard full of bundles and boxes. At the back of the yard, one can see various trees and hear them rustling their leaves. I like the one in the middle because of its height and strong aroma. It's a eucalyptus swaying in the evening breeze, the one blowing in from the lake. A breeze that comes to my uncle's house after having traversed an area circumscribed by cold dry-stone walls, sad dry-stone walls, and farther still, beyond these primitive barriers, dry-stone walls interwoven with 'ichu,' and even more dry-stone walls that have been walked on by lizards and are inhabited by long tailed weasels keeping an eye on their captive rats. Why is it that weasels keep live rats imprisoned in their caves? I know that these rats remain motionless, paralyzed by fear, with a dazed look in their eyes, maybe feeling an icy sensation in their little testicles, as they ponder the day when the weasel will devour their brains in one bite.

Could it be that my uncle called me here because of what I said about killing the second lieutenant? I only mentioned it because that motherfucker went to my house in Conima, one night, broke my face, kicked me in the back, and made me bleed. There was a lot of blood that came out of my mouth; it's the same as when one cuts a chicken's neck. In fact, so much blood came out, that I choked on it. He then locked me away in the guardhouse of his base, hanging from my hands like a slaughtered cow, with my feet immersed in cold water and my bare ass exposed so that his soldiers could laugh at me. It was very humiliating. So, what does my uncle want me to do? Does he want me to bow down before that grunt, and salute him...? What about my manhood? Where's the respect for my age and for the services that I render to my uncle at any given moment...? As soon as he gives me the chance to speak, I'm going to tell him that we need to kill that brat."

Suddenly, my uncle faces me and I take the opportunity that I was waiting for to find some answers: "What's going on Uncle Tomasito? We're acting like madmen: we've changed routes every week and we no longer bring the merchandise across the lake. Why don't we just simply whack that grunt?" I question him with an irritated tone of voice, even though I keep my head down... It could be possible that he'll want to kill me if I show him any sign of disrespect.

As I talk to him, I glue my eyes to the ground next to his feet while I milk the sweat from my fingers, all ten of them, first with one hand, and then with the other. Still talking, I sway my entire body side to side, first putting all my weight on my right foot, then on the left, in a constant but slow manner as if I was moving to the rhythm of the spiritual songs they sing during Sunday mass; I am very afraid and I feel that I am my Uncle's captive. "My dear brother Hilario says that it would be very easy to eliminate him... What do you say to that, Uncle Tomasito?" I ask him as I remain staring at his shoes and dry my sweaty hands by running them through my hair.

My Uncle Tomasito continues to keep ahold of the back of my neck while he walks with me to his back yard. He orders me to take a seat on the stone bench attached to the back wall of his house, and looking down at me he tells me never to bring it up again. "I've been very clear with your brother Hilario and now I am going to be absolutely clear with you," he emphasizes. "No one," he continues, "is going to touch the second lieutenant without my authorization! Something in the wind makes me think that the youngster has a complicated destiny and that whoever thinks of messing with it will make me suffer the consequences.... But this situation with the second lieutenant isn't as serious as it appears to be, nephew. If nobody touches him, I'm certain that his actions in these hills will not change our reality in the slightest bit. The work of this young man is merely symbolic. It's as inconsequential as every day's history. Am I making myself clear?" my uncle says, as he adjusts his grey hat.

My Uncle Tomás speaks with both energy and elegance, dressing his words in a tone of voice that is so sweet that I find it to be hair-raising.... As he mumbles these words, I see his hand traveling in a slow and exasperating manner to grip his Luger...the one that always peers out of his coat pocket. He cocks the pistol as it floats past his face; he watches it with an enraptured look in his eyes as if it were the first time that he'd ever held a gun in his hand. Aunty Evangelina intervenes, shouting something in Aimara, from her bedroom, and my Uncle Tomás, dusting his grey hat on his right knee, answers lovingly: "I'll be finished in a little while, *Mamita* Evangelina. Francisquito is about to leave because he has to return to Conima before it gets too dark."

My uncle turns to me, and I find myself still sitting on the stone bench staring at his gun and breathing with difficulty. "You know very well that I only give orders once, Francisco," he says in a monotonous voice. Then he points the gun in his hand towards his own face. He closes his left eye and with the other looks at the dark orifice, as if he were trying to identify something that was trapped inside that barrel. "Until today, everything has been under control," he utters with disdain, and now squinting with his left eye he lines up the gun's sights to my head and says: "Don't move, nephew. Lift up your head and look me in the eye." He points his Luger at my forehead and makes a noise with his lips that to my ears sound like a slow, tenuous, and diminishing whistle. This noise keeps me motionless and unable to breathe for such a long time that I almost passed out from the lack of oxygen. "Go back to Conima, Francisco Lara," my uncle commands me, "Keep doing your job as you've been ordered to do and may God protect you, nephew," and he says these words in a tone of voice that is so harsh that when I kiss his hand with a reverential bow it makes my blood run cold. I then rush out of his house to traverse the darkness that hangs over the town of Umuchi.

Now, due to my indiscretion with regards to the second lieutenant, my ass is sitting on the bony back of a bow-legged burro that my uncle gave me so that everyone can laugh at me when they see me leave his house hurriedly, staring at the ears of this stupid beast of burden, without daring to look back.

Oh, if I only had the guts to confront my uncle, how different life would be.

RULES OF THE GAME

After finishing his six-month service in the forward operating base of Ninantaya, Second Lieutenant Gerardo Arrieta returned to his MOB in Otábala, on the opposite shore of Lake Titicaca. Feeling blue and suffering from a persecutory delusion that only grew worse as the days went by the young man began to drink almost every evening.

During these many nights of intoxication, Gerardo's faithful drinking companion, Lieutenant Azzarelli, had listened to dozens of accounts of the misfortunes that Arrieta claimed to have suffered while serving in what they both came to call "the hacienda." Since Azzarelli could keep up with the rhythm of his friend's drinking, it became possible for him to learn that Arrieta (thanks to his nocturnal conversations with Eleuterio, the Hacienda's majordomo), had concluded that the group of *colonos* under his authority lived by a bare minimum set of rules, or commandments. What's more, these same *colonos* proclaimed that the esoteric usage of these precepts had been imparted to them by a wise old man who came to the Altiplano centuries before. Although this sage had said very little about either his origins or the strangeness of his physique to the autochthonous dwellers of that tundra, he nonetheless made it be known, with a relative amount of clarity, that he belonged to a tribe of people called the Yu'aos or Ya'ous.

114

The *colonos* couldn't agree with the correct spelling of the tribe's name.

"As to how the Ninantayans pronounce this word", said the second lieutenant, "it is not all together clear to me. I say this because while some of the settlers tend to prolong the sound of the letter 'a' in that blessed name, the others prefer to take the letter 'o' and do the same. Nevertheless, the Ninantayans say that this little visitor had established in his frequent lectures, (or, so it appears), that the Yu'aaaos 'dwelled in a plain located to the south of the town of Ninantaya, at several months' walking distance, just where the bright, wide river of that far-off pampa becomes one with the sea.'"

About the origin of the mysterious traveler himself, the *colonos* had informed Second Lieutenant Arrieta that the old man had arrived on the back of a mule. Furthermore, they insisted that this bizarre sage had come inside a pannier. The young officer said, "They told me that, upon dismounting him from his beast of burden, they were able to confirm that the good man was not only lacking his arms and legs, but that his eyes were cauterized, and the contours of his ears were tucked in and sown to the skin of his cheeks." The oldest men in the fiefdom believed firmly that that needlework had to have been wrought when that sage was still a child, given that his ears were completely welded to the flesh of his visage. The legend also insinuated that the subject in question evoked the image of an immense human egg, due to his being so rotund and limbless, and proposed that he did not elicit, in the least bit, any feelings of fear, violence, or revolt, but rather those of compassion, temperance, and even expectancy. And so, it transpired that the area's residents began to congregate around this oddity at sunset to listen to his sermons and receive his teachings.

* * *

In the face of Lieutenant Azzarelli's resolute line of questioning, Gerardo Arrieta revealed that the inhabitants of Ninantaya had indeed conjectured over the divine origins of the 'egg-man.' They speculate that he must be a god, because otherwise it would have been impossible for him to have mounted his mule and nestled himself within that giant basket in which he had arrived. "Thus the 'Ninantayans,' or if one prefers the 'Ninantayenses,'" said the second lieutenant, "took from this demigod, the four commandments that govern their lives."

The first rule: "never, under any circumstance, demonstrate any sign of bravery." The second rule: "blindly believe that time is circular; that throughout the course of said time, history literally repeats itself, day after day, and therefore the actions that we partake in cannot overlap: 'It is blasphemous to execute two tasks at once; Patience is sweet and Impatience leads to a profound and relentless bitterness.'" The third rule: "any act, no matter how pernicious, atrocious or malevolent it may appear to be, must be considered both good and unanimously acceptable if it promotes the general welfare of the community." The fourth and last rule: "nothing in life is sufficiently attractive or stimulating for any member of the fiefdom to demonstrate any degree of enthusiasm, or effort, to obtain it."

However, what at first glance appeared to be a set of very simple and libertarian commandments, proved to be the basis of a complicated system of regulations. In fact, this becomes evident when one takes into consideration the series of principles that result as derivations, or corollaries, of each one of those four commandments. For example, putting things into one's mouth, with the express purpose of eating them, is a sin, because it demonstrates one's intent to keep on living and thus exhibits a certain level of enthusiasm for wanting to exist. In this case, one is breaking the fourth rule: 'enthusiasm' being the key word.

On the other hand, if one decided to chew coca leaves or gum (if this latter item happened to be available in those pampas) for its own sake, the very act of masticating these items would not be considered an evil deed because in the mind of the Ninantayans this activity was in no way conducive to anything. As such, when viewed from a different angle, eating food constitutes a violation of the second rule. Due to the Ninantayans conception of the circular nature of time, eating and shitting are practically two facets of the same act, and thus in addition to breaking the second divine directive, this action ends up being both disagreeable and disgusting, albeit necessary. Therefore, because of the pressing and unavoidable obligation to keep Life alive, one could opt to nourish oneself in the absence of any witnesses, under the condition that kept one's intake of food to a minimum. With respect to this, the old 'egg-man' promulgated that: "Nothing that a person does in absolute solitude pertains to the reality of the group, for it is only the collective reality that matters for all its members. Any solitary action is tantamount to a fantasy that only exists in the mind of the individual who makes it possible and, thus, it is merely a temptation, and not a sin."

* * *

Arrieta said that he was so astonished by this confusing web of choices that he spent many nights trying to construct a map, or an algorithm as he called it, which was essentially comprised of mathematical tree diagrams representing all the activities that were either, possible, permitted, or prohibited within the rectangle formed by these four commandments. However, on the fourth night, the young officer had become exhausted by this nonsensical philosophical work. And so, he abandoned his project to compose a book of all the regulations (born from these four laws) that he hoped would have helped the hacienda's *colonos* to determine which actions in their lives were permitted and which were not.

The young officer concluded that the people of Ninantaya probably knew only four, eight or perhaps sixteen prohibitions derived from their commandments, due to what he perceived to be their natural inhibition to making any effort, or because they had peacefully surrendered, long ago, to the implacable nature of their reality's daily occurrences. But at the same time, the Ninantayans were busy fabricating stories about how Arrieta had been sinning for four consecutive nights. According to them, he had been trying to demonstrate, with great enthusiasm, that he can create an exhaustive manual on living. They believed that Arrieta found this endeavor emotionally attractive and praiseworthy.

*　*　*

When the second lieutenant talked in his sleep, during his drinking bouts, he tended to narrate his experiences without needing anyone to either question or contradict him.

"I dedicate myself to listening and drinking from time to time," Lieutenant Azzarelli used to say, when any of his friends would ask him about these drinking bouts with the second lieutenant. Meanwhile, Gerardo Arrieta, who was reclining on the bed in his quarters, at the army base in Otábala, would continue to recount the adventures that he'd gotten himself into, during the time that he served on The Hacienda. He said that almost every afternoon, at the end of his day, he would count all the livestock under his care and write down the corresponding figures on the blank sheets of paper in his inventory book. Afterwards, he drank some coffee while smoking a cigarette, and satisfied his curiosity by engaging in long conversations with Eleuterio.

"'Where were the people this morning, when we were going towards the border?' I suddenly asked Eleuterio. 'I didn't see a single soul near any of those houses, whether Christian or animal,' I said to him. This is what I inquired of the majordomo, in an impromptu manner, as if it didn't make much of a difference whether he answered me or not," stammered Second Lieutenant Arrieta while still in a dreamlike trance.

Eleuterio, emerging to the surface of his consciousness, as eager and happy as a dolphin jumping out of the water, responded: "Sleeping, Jefecito. Well, they were waiting for the sun to warm up the day. We are inside your house, taitita, and even you are wearing your chullo."

"You mean they're still in bed at eight-thirty in the morning?" said Arrieta as he took off his chullo and scratched his head, his hair pasted to his scalp due to his prolonged use of that typical Andean headwear.

Eleuterio answered: "Well, at eight-thirty it's still too cold outside for bodies that are so skinny, Jefecito. At nine-thirty they get out of bed of course, *taitita*, and from there they head out to tend to their allotted chores on the hacienda, *Jefecitooo.*"

"They don't eat any breakfast first?"

"Of course, they do *taititaaa.*"

"What do they eat?"

"A little soup, of course *Jefecitoooo.* A little bit of water; *cochallullo*;[23] a few grains of rice; dried maize kernels; and a *chuño* for each family member, *papacitooo,*" said Eleuterio. As he delivered his words wrapped in an anguished tone, he gesticulated with all five fingers of his hand, his fingertips bunched together, as if he were trying to compare their misery to the dimensions of a tick. He

---

[23] A type of algae that grows in little ponds found among the hills of the Altiplano.

119

accompanied this mimicry by giving the last vowel, of the last two words that he uttered a vast and mournful tone: "Their portions are that *smaaall, Jefecitooo*."

"Is that all?"

"That's all they get to eat in these parts, *taitita*," Eleuterio said, looking at the ground and shaking his head like the pendulum on a grandfather-clock.

"And what do they eat at noon?"

"They just have another bowl of soup, Second Lieutenant."

"The same as they had for breakfast?"

"Well, yes, *Jefecito*. I already told you several times; that's all that one has to eat around here."

"At what time of day?"

"At what time of the day what, *patroncito*?" Eleuterio said with a smile, as if he'd only just begun to take part in the dialogue that they had been having.

"Don't be a wise-ass! At what time of the day do they eat this second helping of soup that you're telling me about?!" the Second Lieutenant roared as he struck his fist against the tabletop.

"At four o'clock in the evening, *Viracocha*[24]; the hour at which their day begins to drowse, before they make their way back home. Do you understand *papacito*?" said Eleuterio hastily, with fear shining in his eyes.

"You are a big smart-ass, Eleuterio!" the second lieutenant answered. "Now it turns out that, if I take your last reply into consideration, I'm the one who's the dumbass in this dialogue! What I want to know is: How do these

---

[24] Viracocha is considered the most important deity of the Incan and pre-Incan cultures. The natives depicted him as a white man, of medium height, dressed in a white tunic with a belt tied around his waist, and a book in his hand. He is the creator of the universe, the equivalent of the Christian God, i.e. "The Father".

people nourish themselves? When do they eat a *real* meal? I mean a real meal, with meat and potatoes. Is this fucking fasting due to yet another one of the egg-man's commandments?"

"No, *papitoooo*, the *Huevito*[25] ate with us, not much, but he ate."

"Are you going to fucking answer me, wise-ass? How do these people nourish themselves?"

"Don't get angry, *papitoooo*," said Eleuterio, once again elongating the last vowel sound of each final word in a plaintive tone. "That's what little food they have, *taititaaaa*. They always eat just that and never ask for more. The people here are content to live like that."

"And how is it that you, Eleuterio, always get up early and go wherever I go?"

"Well, *Viracocha*, I nourish myself everyday with the same beans and potatoes that your troops eat."

"And is it true, Eleuterio, that the rest of your people aren't hungry at all?" said Arrieta, as he stopped smoking and drinking his coffee.

"Well, they chew coca leaves, *papitooo*. No hunger. No problems. Sleeping and resting is all that their body asks of them, *señorcito*," Eleuterio said extending his arms as if he were on a cross, in the way in which the Aimaras are accustomed to doing whenever they want to reinforce what they are saying. And all the while, Eleuterio had been standing in front of the second lieutenant, with his feet together, and his head half-lowered, tilted slightly to the left.

---

[25] The diminutive, or term in endearment, in Spanish for "egg"

AND WHAT IF THERE WERE NO GOD?

When Second Lieutenant Gerardo Arrieta received the brutal impact of a club to the anterior middle of his right thigh, he realized that he was losing consciousness. A sharp and lengthy sound, like the striking of an anvil, burrowed into his ears and invaded his entire being. The young officer could never tell for how long he had been a prisoner of that sensation, but as the noise in his ears began to dissipate, he had the presentiment that he was coming back to his body after having lost his life.

At that point, Arrieta began to draw strength from the rage that this premonition produced in him. Experiencing an acute pain in his forehead, he focused his mind on this source of affliction, relaxed the muscles of his thorax, and tried to reason. Gerardo could verify that his brain was an empty cave and the only thoughts that were possible for him to conjure up at this stage were all related to the agonizing pain in his thigh. He could hear a series of violent shouts in Aimara and he had the certainty that he was sitting on a cold stone floor with his eyes shrouded in darkness.

Gradually, he discovered that a breeze was beginning to inundate his lungs. He enjoyed that extreme cold air of the Altiplano that he had cursed so many times before, while he was patrolling the border, because it froze his ears and nose.

Almost without realizing it, he began to perceive his surroundings. At first, he could only see a pale yellowish color; then the reality before his eyes took on a vaporous shade of grey, until, as the seconds went by, everything eventually acquired a normal appearance. At that instant, he imagined that the sky was a dark ocean full of miniature fluorescent buoys and discovered that the individual who had attacked him was only six feet away. This man wore a dark poncho and a bright, blood red, and provocative *chullo*.

Arrieta opened his mouth attempting to shout an invective; call all his troops; or ask for help from his orderly, Private Quispe, but he was unable to emit anything other than a muffled, guttural roar. To give himself the necessary strength, he swallowed some saliva and anxiously coated his lungs with the frozen air as many times as he could. He cleared his head, tried to draw up a new inventory of thoughts, and to his satisfaction discovered that it was possible for him to entertain four concurrent ideas. 1) Someone hit my leg; 2) The man that is shouting at me in an offensive manner is my attacker; 3) my "Fat Trickster" is behind my back and is lodged in the sheath hanging from my belt, at the level of my kidneys; 4) my primary objective is to stick this "fat" dagger in my attacker's calf.

Before he could strike back, the second lieutenant decided to unhinge his enemy by taunting him. He thought that this would not only reduce the effectiveness of any future blow, but it would also allow him to distract his enemy enough to facilitate the extraction of his dagger. And so, Gerardo began to hurl a series of insults, each one more aggressive than the last, and in between these invectives he dared his attacker to put him out of his misery: "Come here, you *cholo* motherfucker; finish me off!" he said. "Come closer, you faggot! Finish what you've started!"

Feeling increasingly in control of his body and his brain, the young officer continued his vituperation while he remained seated on the flagstone floor. Ostensibly using his left hand to rub the impacted area on his leg, Arrieta covertly placed his right hand at the height of his tailbone close to his short dagger. The second lieutenant knew that this cold weapon, due to the shape of its blade and lack of a fuller, was going to be difficult to pull out of wherever he happened to bury it.

Arrieta's attacker smiled and shouted at his victim in Aimara. Clutched in his left hand, and resting against his shoulder, was a four-foot-long eucalyptus branch. In the face of the jeers and taunts of the young officer on the floor, the man with the red chullo made up his mind. Grabbing his cudgel with both hands, he raised it high enough to put him in the best possible position to deliver the finishing blow to his victim's head. At this point, he said distinctly in Spanish, "Look at me, you little shit, I'm going to send you to the afterlife!"

* * *

Second Lieutenant Gerardo Arrieta had always doubted the existence of God. Ever since he was a little boy, in the first years of elementary school, he used to lose himself in thoughts about if there was indeed an all-powerful being, capable of rewarding people by sending them to Heaven, or punishing them by casting them down to Hell. The Christian Brothers at the La Salle School, in his hometown of Arequipa, suffered many headaches trying to answer his questions. "If God is good, I mean really good, Brother Fermin, how is it possible that He would send me to Hell for eternity just because of some insignificant sin that I've committed?" he asked one day when he was in fifth grade. The child never wanted to hear or understand the explanations that the good brother gave him. Little Gerardo would just shake his head as a sign of denial. However, after a while, he confessed to Brother Fermín that even when

124

he was feverishly at prayer, he needed to close his eyes and clench his fists because it was at this moment that an immense feeling of doubt would come over him like a gust of wind, swirling the sacred verses about him as debris caught in a tornado.

Upon being admitted to the military academy in Lima, at the age of eighteen, Cadet Arrieta resumed his practice of fervent and dedicated prayer. During the sporadic weekends in which he could go out and see his family, he would tell them that without prayer he would have never survived the hard life of that academy. Yet, at the same time, Arrieta's peers were fully aware that that he enjoyed frequently engaging in lengthy and tortuous discussions with them wherein he would try to demonstrate the nonexistence of God. He proposed to them that it should be blatantly obvious to any member of the armed forces that God was an entity incompatible with war. They could not, as soldiers, both serve their country through acts of war, and, at the same time, serve God, who demanded love, peace, and the need to turn the other cheek in the face of any attack.

Arrieta never wanted to accept the solid reasons the officers gave him when they explained that even in the Bible one could find, and clearly read, how there are certain circumstances wherein God propitiates, encourages, and participates in war with his divine protection. Arrieta merely contemplated those officers with an air of petulance and replied: "What you guys are saying doesn't make any sense at all. In theory, God is perfect and infinitely good. Aren't you able to comprehend the meaning of the word, *infinite*?" And upon reaching this dialectical crossroad, Cadet Arrieta would hastily leave these meetings without further commentary, grinning on one side of his mouth.

The young man would behave in this way because these conversations, instead of dissipating his doubts, only served to amplify his existential anguish. He didn't know whether to pray and cry out for God's forgiveness, or to go forth and proclaim the nonexistence of the Lord at the top of his lungs.

* * *

Once he heard that last threatening and apparently definitive phrase made in Spanish by his attacker, the second lieutenant lifted his face and could see how the man with the red *chullo* began to raise the club that he held in his hands. Arrieta's mind began to fill with images at such a speed that that fraction of a second in his life seemed like an eternity. Perceiving the rancid odor that emanates from the greasy wool of recently shorn sheep; the stench of *cañazo*, all-too-common among the Indians of that region; and the aroma of coca leaves mixed with saliva, the young officer concluded that his attacker was inebriated, high on coca, and had on a recently woven poncho.

He contemplated the individual standing over him and could compare him with the image of his papa in the horrendous act of killing a rabid dog with an axe handle, in the patio of his house, in Ocoña, his papa's hometown. Nonetheless, the second lieutenant was also able to sense the series of imperative commands that his brain was sending him. He needed to pull his "fat" dagger out of its sheath, raise it to the level of his ear, then even further, behind the line of his shoulders, and thrust his hand forward, as fast as an arrow, towards the thickest part of his attacker's calf muscle.

And so, wounded and sitting on the cold stone floor of the Peruvian Altiplano, the young officer buried the resplendent, conic steel blade in the leg of the man who stood before him. After witnessing this action, a nearby barn owl launched its ear-piercing shriek into the darkest recesses of the night. The officer's attacker then dropped his cudgel on the floor behind him. He groaned as if he'd been hit in the solar plexus. As he moved back, he jumped up and down repeatedly on his good leg and bent down to try to extract the sharp object from his body with both hands. When he realized that he was not going to be able to pull the blade out in the way he was intending, he sat down on the floor. He let out a loud cry that frightened the vizcachas, the long-tailed weasels, and even the wild guinea pigs that lived between the cracks in the dry-stone wall that surrounded Arrieta's house. It was a horrendous howl and Arrieta was more afraid of it than of the threat against his life to which he had been subjected just a few minutes before. In that moment of confusion, the second lieutenant remembered that he had a pistol hanging from his belt. With some difficulty, he unbuttoned the holster, took out his Browning and indiscriminately began to fire. As he had not yet been able to regain full control over his arms, the bullets flew in various directions minus the one in which the individual with the dagger in his leg was to be found. After the fourth shot, the second lieutenant could see how the criminal limped around a corner and sought protection behind his house as he proceeded to flee under the cover of darkness.

The bellow emitted by the man with the red *chullo* served as a clarion call for all the inhabitants of the hamlet. No sooner had this roar ceased than the night air encompassing Arrieta began to be populated with sounds. Soon one could hear the stomping of the soldiers' boots against the floor as they ran back towards their base and the officer's quarters. To the beat of this thumping noise, the second lieutenant heard a rustle of voices giving the alarm intermingled with a plethora of profanities. His men had noticed something out of the ordinary and were now in a hurry to try and correct this snafu, whatever it may be.

* * *

Cadet Arrieta's existential anguish grew over time and drove him to a complete agnosticism. His difficult childhood, in Arequipa, combined with the unorthodox upbringing of the Aimara-speaking maidservants that took care of him in his younger and more vulnerable years, had filled him with fears by day and apocalyptic terrors by night. Even during his years in the Academy, the cadet frequently suffered from one particularly frightening nightmare that would awaken him around three-in-the-morning and leave him with the sensation that he was only able to open and move his eyes. Although the certainty of his imminent death was the focal point of this malignant dream, the young man had the illusion that if he fought hard enough to wake up, if he could at least manage to move his arms and legs, if in the end it were only possible for him to leap out of bed to feel the cold tiled floor with the soles of his bare feet, his passage into the next life could be avoided. What was terrifying about this experience was that when he opened his eyes he could recognize the door-less entry of his bedroom and the corridor in front of it as in waking life. At that moment, he felt inundated with the conviction that Satan himself was coming for his soul and that eventually, he'd infiltrate his room through that concrete doorframe and approach his bed. That night, the nightmare reached its climax when Arrieta heard the echo of boot-heels approaching the entrance of his room. It was the cadet on night-watch duty calmly and attentively walking up and down the one-hundred-meter corridor outside the dorm rooms of all the cadets. The reason for this repetitive nocturnal march of his was, in theory, to maintain "discipline" among his supposedly sleeping comrades by making sure that none of them were smoking, masturbating, or simply conversing with one another.

In the face of that syncopated series of prolonged sounds that kept growing louder with each step that the night-guard took, our young man perspired (because of the intolerable fear produced by his nightmare), paralyzed in his bed, until his pajamas, sheets, and pillow case, were completely moistened with sweat. And so, when the night-guard stopped at the entryway of Arrieta's dorm room, Gerardo could see a shadow outlined by the corridor's dying light, and he would suddenly sit up to breathe desperately as if someone had been holding his mouth and nose closed for a long time.

In fact, Arrieta *was* seeing the Devil standing before him, but at the same time, he was conscious that he had everything under control because he had finally awakened. It was only when the cadet on guard duty, standing in the entryway of his room, started to say, "What's wrong with you, dumbass? Lie down and get some rest! It's 0:300! You can still sleep for a couple more hours!" that his heart rate would finally begin to slow down. At this point, Arrieta would thank his fellow cadet, and go back into the sack. He covered his head with his blanket and pondered the fact that if the Devil existed then the most rational proposition to complete this equation would be to accept the existence of God as a counterweight. But just as soon as he finished processing this thought in his brain, the same old doubt would return since he, after a few seconds of darkness under his blanket, would come to understand that the person appearing at the entryway of his dorm was just the night-guard cadet and not the dreaded Satan himself.

At the end of each of these adventures, the lack of any concrete proof compelled him to return to his initial agnosticism.

* * *

By the time the troops under the second lieutenant's command finally arrived at the front of his house, Arrieta's right thigh had swollen to the size of a watermelon. The hematoma was so extensive that it stretched the fabric of his fatigue pants to the point that it looked like the second lieutenant was wearing a leotard. All Arrieta's troops who arrived on the scene had astonished looks on their faces. Some of them put their hands on their cheeks, as if they were looking at something out of this world. One or two cried uncontrollably like children who had lost both parents. Others, their eyes as wide as headlights, made a noise that sounded like an accidentally punctured beach ball that was rapidly losing all its air supply.

The first one of these men to react in a coherent manner was Leoncio Quispe, Arrieta's orderly.

"It's all my fault, Pops," he said between sobs.

"We're all to blame," added the medic, Sergeant Valdés. Suddenly their lamentations and comments turned into a despicable uproar where the only thing that one could make out was that everyone felt guilty about what had happened to their commander. Then the second lieutenant shouted as he called his men to order and told them that none of them was responsible for what had happened.

"I was the one who, like an idiot, made the mistake of having ventured outside to contemplate the beauty of the stars as if I were in my house in Lima," he said between groans and deep breaths of fresh air, as if these would in some way mitigate his pain. "Let's not waste time. I think he may have broken my femur and if we don't do something quick I'm going to die," he added as he winced with pain and exhaled profusely.

Arrieta was conscious of the fact that his garrison had neither a radio to call for help nor a vehicle with which to evacuate him. He was frighteningly aware of the almost complete isolation in which he and his soldiers found themselves.

By ten o'clock that night, the soldiers were walking from room to room like robots. They came and went from the second lieutenant's bedroom to his kitchen, crossing the living and dining rooms along the way. None of them uttered a word; they just marched to-and-fro, scanning the floor as if looking for mines, without thinking about anything or anyone else. The only one who continued to express himself, and in a loud, bellowing voice, was the young officer who appeared to be in a delirious state. Arrieta made strange requests. He ordered Quispe to recover his "Fat Trickster" which was to be found buried in the leg of his attacker. He babbled that the dogs were barking a terrible omen, to which the orderly replied: "There are no dogs in this area, Pops. There's nothing for them to eat in these barren pampas." The second lieutenant was incapable of processing any rational explanations. He muttered that the man who busted up his leg was, without a doubt, the Devil incarnate.

"They tricked us by offering us a whore for free, sir." Valdés suddenly said to Arrieta. He explained to him that at five o'clock in the evening on that fateful day, when all the soldiers were resting in the barracks, the town's telegraph operator arrived to bring some "good news." The telegrapher told the medic that an affable Bolivian truck driver had paid for a prostitute "so that each *soldadito*[26] stationed in FOB Ninantaya could purge himself of that manhood which he had been accumulating over the past few months and should be like toothpaste by now." Valdés related that he and his comrades immediately seized upon this long-awaited opportunity and stampeded to the town. He added that they all quickly gave into the joys of carnal pleasure, but in so doing "they made sure to form a line with the utmost discipline," until each man had had his turn. After this, Valdés stopped talking. He covered his face with his hands and, speaking through the interstices between his fingers, said: "What a tragedy! When I heard that howl of pain that sounded like it was coming from either an animal

---

[26] Soldado: Spanish for soldier; soldadito, is the diminutive for soldado.

or the Devil himself, a light bulb went off inside my head: I came to realize that something bad, very bad, had occurred in our absence. That horrendous cry was an evil omen." He then added that at that moment he remembered the second lieutenant's words as they played back incessantly in his mind. "No one will ever give you anything for free. If someone can offer you any valuables, at no cost at all, it is because he definitely expects something in return."

And so, it was at that hour of the night that Yatiri suddenly appeared among them. All those present turned around at the same time to contemplate the smiling old man standing in the threshold of Arrieta's room. He came laden with several small bags, just like the one in which he always carried his coca leaves.

"He looks like an equeco[27]," said the orderly, Quispe, while biting the nail of his index finger.

"He's Eleuterio's father," corrected Sergeant Valdés.

"What does that piece of shit old man want now?" complained Corporal Huallpa as he rubbed his hands against his pant-legs.

Grinning from ear to ear, Yatiri had entered the second lieutenant's house as if it were his own. Without any hesitation, he walked straight to the dining room table. He began to sing a litany in Aimara and summoned Private Leoncio Quispe, pronouncing his name with such clarity that it seemed as if he were speaking perfect Spanish. Arrieta's orderly hesitantly approached the old man. Yatiri placed his bony hand on the back of Quispe's neck, and after looking intently into his eyes, he mumbled a series of words in the orderly's ear. Although Quispe understood some Aimara, with which he managed to get by, he had felt that

---

[27] A clay figurine depicting a smiling fat man, with open arms, loaded with diminutive packages containing groceries and all kinds of presents and which the people of Peru believe propitiates prosperity and affluence; this term comes from the Aimara word *Iqiqu*, which is the name this people gave to their god of abundance.

the message the old man had poured into his ear had seeped directly into the very core of his brain as if it were spoken in his native Quechua. The soldier turned around and headed towards the kitchen. Shortly thereafter, Quispe and Yatiri walked to the side of Arrieta's bed, loaded with pots, a frying pan, and a brazier full of coal, which were the utensils required by the old man minutes before.

* * *

After graduating from the military academy in Lima, Arrieta was stationed in the military base of Otabala, on the western shore of Lake Titicaca. When he first arrived in the Altiplano, his nightmare underwent a metamorphosis. Whether this transformation was, as he believed, a byproduct of the area's high elevation and the fact that in Otabala a multitude of unfamiliar officers and soldiers surrounded him, little by little, he noticed that his terrifying dream was becoming clearer. Now the Devil, who had persecuted him for most of his short life, had an Indian's face, was very young, and at times spoke to him as if he were his friend. This bewildered the young second lieutenant. The nightly experience felt unmistakably real. Arrieta was unable to differentiate dream from reality. One night, two months after arriving in Otabala, Arrieta's anguish became unbearable. The fear that plagued him grew to the point that when he woke up, drenched in sweat, he jumped out of bed and shouted: "There is no God! The Devil doesn't exist, and if he shows his face around here, I'm going to kill him!" At that precise moment, his orderly, Leoncio Quispe, who was entering the room, carrying his commanding officer's recently shined riding boots, naively laughed and butt in saying: "Who are you going to kill, Sir?"

From that evening on, the second lieutenant spent his nights in an extremely dangerous manner. He acquired the custom of going to bed fully dressed in his combat fatigues, with an M1911 pistol in his right hand, and a Japanese Type 97 fragmentation hand grenade in his left. Arrieta had become a ticking time bomb. Every time he awoke from one of his demonic nightmares, he was ready either to detonate his World War II relic, or fire his .45 caliber hand gun in the dead of night. Nevertheless, when Gerardo Arrieta received orders from his military base in Otabala to take charge of the Ninantaya Hacienda, his nightmares gave way to a series of bucolic dreams. In them, the dreaded Satan gave way to a benevolent shepherd. This good man, covered with a vicuña-hide poncho, forced the young Arrieta to walk among his sheep. This fellow, whose age Arrieta was unable to determine, treated him as if he were one more member of the herd; he neither mistreated nor denied the second lieutenant food. On the contrary, despite considering him just another ruminant, the mysterious shepherd shared his food with him.

As soon as Yatiri was ready to begin his ritual healing, he spoke in a ceremonious manner and with a grave tone of voice. The curandero only addressed Private Leoncio Quispe. He expressed himself in Aimara: *Jichhurust aka luriyamasti, Jichhurusti Jisukristu juma Awkuir juma Taykaru*...and kept going for five minutes in what sounded like a Japanese version of a Catholic prayer. The old man then stopped talking, closed his eyes, and with his right hand, he traced an imaginary line from Quispe's chest to Arrieta's solar plexus. The orderly explained to the second lieutenant that the shaman was requesting his fellow soldiers to tie him to his bed. "The second lieutenant's hands need to be tied to the iron tubes on the bunk's headboard and his feet need to be secured to the ones on the footboard," explicated the accidental interpreter, so that the others would follow suit.

"Give me my pistol so I can kill him!" shouted Arrieta. His faithful orderly then explained to him with the utmost clarity that Yatiri was the only one who could save his life.

"He is the witch doctor of this fiefdom, Pops," Quispe said. "In this little world of ours, he, and no one else but he, can cure you."

By three AM the following morning, the second lieutenant was sleeping peacefully. Yatiri had applied a poultice to the swollen area of his right thigh and had bandaged his leg with bed sheets (which he had asked Quispe to cut into long strips) from the groin, or as Yatiri called it, "the flank," to the tip of his toes. The medicine man prepared his poultice by throwing into the hot frying pan various leaves, with which Quispe and his companions were unfamiliar; white sugar; a few teeth from a long-tailed weasel; the heart of a kestrel; the tip of a vizcachas tail; and a brown liquid extracted from the dried uterus of a vicuña. Lastly, he spits into the frying pan a mixture of chewed up coca leaves and *cañazo* that he had been accumulating between his teeth and his cheeks.

Arrieta cried out during the first hour as he tried to free his hands and feet from the well-secured ligatures made by his soldiers. Later, he begged them, for half an hour, to scratch his leg since he could no longer stand that terrible itch. Yatiri, with a smile on his lips, said no; that none of them should dare to scratch the young man's injured leg because that could form an open wound in Arrieta's leg and that would mean the end of his life. Finally, the incapacitated officer fell asleep. When the smiling sun appeared to show his face, Arrieta awoke and noticed that Yatiri was so close to his nose that he could count the number of wrinkles on the old man's visage. He could even smell the stench of *cañazo* coming from his mouth, and felt the softness of his fingers wiping the sweat from his forehead.

In the days that followed this initial healing session, Yatiri spoke with Arrieta non-stop. The second lieutenant listened with rapt attention and without protest, from rosy-fingered sunrise to pale red sunset. The medic, Sgt. Valdés, asked his commanding officer how it was possible for him to understand Yatiri, if the old man only spoke Aimara. The young officer, with a serious look on his face, responded: "I don't have the slightest fucking idea, but somehow, in my mind, I completely understood everything he said."

Six days after Arrieta was cunningly attacked, he was finally able to get out of bed. Eventually, with the help of a rustic crutch, made by Quispe under the direction of the curandero, he began to walk by himself. Yatiri never left his side and all this time he spoke to him with the persistence of a prisoner on death-row requesting to be pardoned. He would jump about to place himself in front of his patient to converse with him in a loud voice, and then skip over to his side, perhaps to tell him more important things in a low voice, but close to the officer's ear.

The soldiers were sure that the young Arrieta had changed completely after his infirmity. "He's talked too much with that crazy old man," they said with a worried look in their eyes and, shaking their heads, they added that: "Nothing good can come from these chats. That crafty fucker is going to put him in danger and then what are we going to do?"

It took two months for the second lieutenant to walk as well as he did before that malignant night's attack. Quispe says that the bond between his commander and Yatiri was

136

very deep. That the second lieutenant had told him that
while he was bedridden, the shaman had taken him by the
hand to the town of Umuchi, to show him the house of his
attacker. "Hilario's his name," Arrieta said that the old man
confided to him. Gerardo told Quispe that the shaman
added: "It is imperative that you know this house by heart
so that when the time comes you'll be ready to kill that devil
incarnate." After his convalescence had ended, Arrieta said:
"I can finally get a tranquil night's rest. I know now who

the devil is. Yatiri has shown me his house. Satan can
no longer scare me. From here on out, I'm the one who's
going to be haunting him in his dreams."

LEONCIO AND HIS 'POPS'

Private Leoncio Quispe, a rifleman in the Peruvian Cavalry, is Second Lieutenant Arrieta's orderly. This jovial and rotund *cholo* calls his boss "Pops." It's because Quispe's biological father died when he was just four years old. From that moment on, his oldest maternal uncle took charge of his education. The small orphan learned the chores pertaining to both field and kitchen while attentively contemplating a sharp and flexible branch in his uncle's hand, which, at his slightest mistake, made him feel an intense, burning pain across his back. For some mysterious reason, when this young boy came into his own, he developed the sweetest and happiest of dispositions. Nonetheless, Private Quispe's eyes were always wide awake so that he could observe with an attention as sharp as his kitchen knife, anyone who came too close to him. Leoncio clearly remembered that, before he had reached puberty, someone, who was always within an arm's length of him, had constantly checkered his back with the finest of scars.

But, despite everything, Private Quispe didn't hold a grudge against his uncle. Leoncio says that his mother's older brother had frequently told him that if he had ever mistreated him in any way, it was only meant for his dear nephew's own good.

During this last week, without ever losing his joyful and loquacious nature, Leoncio Quispe became increasingly preoccupied with the mental health of his boss. His "Pops," as he likes to call the second lieutenant, is exhibiting the signs of a mourner. This precarious situation demanded all Leoncio's attention because not too long ago the officer had been more of a friend than a superior officer. To tell the truth, no one in the military detachment at Ninantaya can venture a guess as to why, lately, the young second lieutenant has been behaving so strangely.

* * *

In the area around the hamlet of Conima, on the shores of Lake Titicaca, lives Francisco Lara, an elementary school teacher who encourages left wing ideas. Every morning, the good Francisco devotes himself to the task of what he calls "de-stupefying kids." He calls it that because of the amount of effort he must exert in teaching the three Rs to the children of the various fiefdoms that surround the school where he is the only teacher. Nonetheless, Francisco believes himself to be an 'orthodox' teacher. He says that his best 'teaching assistant' in the school is a broom stick that he keeps next to the chalkboard. "These snot-nosed brats rub their heads and recite the alphabet by heart any time I feint that I'm going to ask my 'assistant' for his help."

Every afternoon, and during the greater part of every night, Francisco dedicates himself to activities that are not only far more thrilling, but also riskier. Three times a week, 'Professor Lara' helps his Uncle Tomás Ccañato, a man of great authority in that region. Tomás is a man whom the people of the region call 'the Ghost,' though they do so in hushed tones so that no one else will hear. In accompanying his uncle, the 'professor,' can both make some extra cash "for the sake of the cause" as he likes to call it, and smuggle a few handguns, from Bolivia, which will later be sold in the highlands around Cuzco.

* * *

The most important changes in Second Lieutenant Arrieta's demeanor transpired a few days after someone killed Eleuterio, the majordomo of the Ninantaya Hacienda. Quispe said that his "Pops" stopped sharing his daily plans with him, as was his custom every dinnertime. "This change in my 'Pops' routine," whispered the orderly, "began three days after Eleuterio's funeral." During those seventy-two hours, the second lieutenant still spoke with Quispe and even told him that he hadn't been sleeping at all at night. "I'm only able to nod off, Quispecito," said the young officer. "I fill my bed with pillows so that it seems as if I'm sleeping in my bed and I sit on the saddle that I have on the floor in the corner of my bedroom. There, with a gun in my hand and aiming it at the door all the time, I nod off *cholo*; I'm only able to nod off throughout the night," said Arrieta. Quispe, being the chatterbox that he is, insinuated to his "Pops" that no one in that Altiplano wanted to kill them, because they were, after all, members of the army, and as such, they had guns at their disposal. The second lieutenant answered his orderly, with a calm and serious demeanor, that therein was the danger. He added that it was those very guns, which Quispe mentioned, that those bandits were trying to obtain. He explained to Leoncio, that the machine gun they had in Ninantaya was, in the eyes of those sons-of-bitches, like a pot of honey to a swarm of flies. The young officer also confided to his orderly that he himself was a victim of fear, "You shouldn't believe for one second that I am invulnerable to that shit." Arrieta tried explaining to Private Quispe that the anguish accumulating in his guts was like an animal squirming in his stomach, and impeding his breathing; that that incessant sensation produced a pain in his chest. "I think that the only way to eliminate this feeling, that I have inside of me, is for me to leave here abruptly, in the middle of the night, go to their houses, surprise them in their sleep, and then club them and kick them to death. That way they'll learn to never plot any more massacres or assaults on my turf."

*   *   *

Sergeant Gregorio Valdés, the squad's medic, awoke upon feeling a hand exerting a brutal amount of force on his mouth to keep him from shouting. In the pitch-black darkness of the house where the soldiers slept, the medic came to believe that he was living through a nightmare since it had become so difficult for him to breathe. It seemed as if his sternum had stuck to his spine and that he was on the verge of death. Stretched out on his camp bed, and unable to move, he saw his commander's visage, that of Second Lieutenant Arrieta, illuminated by a small flashlight that the officer held towards his own face. Gregorio remained motionless and took in only a minimal quantity of air at a time. The vision of his boss' face calmed him down considerably, especially when Arrieta, removing his hand from over the medic's mouth, signaled him to remain silent by crossing his index finger over his own lips.

The Second Lieutenant, who had been sitting on the medic's chest, got up and proceeded to kneel on the floor next to him. Valdés listened as his boss whispered instructions into his ear. From what he heard, the sergeant understood that he was to get dressed in absolute silence, bundle up as best as he could because it was very cold outside, put on his black balaclava, take up his rifle, and leave the soldiers' barracks to make his way towards his commander's quarters. "The magazines loaded with live rounds of ammunition are in my room," the officer had mumbled upon giving his instructions. Sergeant Valdés felt a lump form in his throat upon hearing the phrase "live rounds" intermingled with the last words spoken by his commander, and he tasted that feeling of agony that is born of fear.

Minutes later, and in a similar manner, Privates Cusiskka and Sulla were forced to live through the intense emotions that Valdés had already experienced minutes before, when they opened their eyes and saw before them the irradiated outline of Second Lieutenant Arrieta's face.

* * *

Francisco Lara felt the weight of his front door as it fell on top of him and crushed him against the floor. The view that he possessed of his belongings within his abode darkened; he ceased to perceive his rickety old bed and the sheep skins that were entangled with his blankets, the cardboard boxes stacked against the walls, and the clay pot on the adobe cook stove, boiling water. It was five o'clock in the morning, and he had barely finished his monthly task of preparing a shipment of used handguns, when he was rained on by a series of kicks, thrusts, and rifle butts. He tried to defend himself (it was not courage that he was lacking), but the suddenness of the attack had been such that he was unable to put his thoughts together. For a moment, he just let things take their course. The blows and shouts penetrated him from all four corners like ice cold stiletto knives that cut through to his very bones.

When Francisco became conscious of the reality of his situation, he stood up, raised his right fist, and shouted with a stentorian voice to condemn the outrage, the barbarity of that military action that was being perpetrated against him, and to demand that he be treated with the proper respect due to a school teacher. The attackers contemplated him with a look of disdain and laughed at him, repeatedly calling him a 'dumbass!' as they wagged their index fingers at him. When 'Professor' Lara invoked the articles of the Constitution, the leader of his assailants defiantly approached him with his rifle raised in the air, the butt pointing at the school teacher, and giving a delirious howl, he violently sent his weapon crashing against Francisco's face. The skin stretched over his cheekbone opened like an enormous buttonhole. The victim didn't feel any pain. If anything, he felt a chill that made his body tremble from his head down to his toes, and sensed how a slight feeling of nausea lodged itself in his solar plexus. The school teacher then fell on his back, received many a kick as he rolled about on the dirt floor and now, in the stockade of the army base in Rucano, as he speaks with his lawyers, he remembers a riot of shouts, the guffaws of his attackers, and the salty taste of his own fresh blood against his tongue.

Valdés comments to Quispe that their boss may have gone a little overboard that early morning in Conima. "He gave it to that poor school teacher pretty hard, even when he fell down and began to drag himself across the floor," says the sergeant to the private, gesticulating wildly with his hands. "I thought that he was going to die on us, Leoncio. I even had to stitch up his face because your 'Pops' hit him so hard with the butt of his rifle that he left a gash on his cheekbone so wide it looked as if the prisoner had a second mouth," tells Valdés in an almost whispering tone of voice. Upon hearing this, Private Quispe put forth a fiery defense of his boss. He tried to explain to the medic that that's how war is, and that only those who strike first, and use the most force, can come out alive in the end. And so, by acting in this violent manner, his 'Pops,' the commander of the Ninantaya detachment, was only demonstrating his serious concern for the welfare and lives of all his men. But Valdés replies: "But we're not even at war, Leoncio, so what are you talking about? You weren't there Leoncio, I was. The man our boss attacked last night is merely a school teacher..."

Arrieta's orderly stands up, and extending his right arm to put his hand on the sergeant's shoulder (as is the habit of the second lieutenant), looks him in the eye and says to him: "And the weapons, the revolvers, and the boxes full of documents that all of you confiscated from his house? What were those for? Did he need all those things to teach the children how to read? My 'Pops' says that in those very documents it was outlined, in detail, how they planned to kill all of us." Valdés remains silent for a few seconds before asking one last question. "Don't you think, Leoncio, that it would have been more reasonable for us to tie his hands in front, with a rope, and let him walk as we dragged him to our stockade, instead of bringing him here lying prone across the back of a burro, coughing up blood and barely breathing?"

Two months later, Second Lieutenant Arrieta comes walking out of his house with the help of a crude cane to receive two captains who have arrived at his door. The young officer drags, to the best of his ability, his apparently wounded right leg. He greets his superior officers and, with a grimace that evinces his pain, inquires of them the reason for such a strange visit. Not once, during the previous five months, had any of his uniformed colleagues deemed it necessary to pay him any social calls. Ninantaya, to put it bluntly, is just a four-house town. It's a damned puna in which the snakes crawl in slow motion because they're freezing to death and where nothing grows other than ichu, potatoes, quinoa, and cañihua.

The captains speak as if they were twins who hail from another planet; they each pronounce a phrase, one after the other, to complete a single idea. They explain to Arrieta that they have come in search of the followers of one Francisco Lara, a subversive whom the second lieutenant had held prisoner and later sent to the army base in Rucano, months before. Gerardo Arrieta smiles, despite the pain that he feigns in his face, and with his right arm stretched out points west at a jaggedly cut horizon, saying: "In the direction towards which I'm indicating, at three hours walking distance, is located Conima. It's a little hamlet on the shores of Lake Titicaca and there, in the surroundings of that community, in a tiny school, you'll be able to find information about the individual you mentioned."

In talking to the captains, the young officer neglects to mention that to walk in that puna it's necessary to wear rubber boots, to minimize the risk of breaking one's ankles. "As you can see, I can hardly get around," he says to them. "I have a bum leg and as such I can't accompany you." The captains, disconcerted by this news, inform the second lieutenant that, thanks to the diligence on the part of a team of human rights lawyers from the city of Puno, the commander of the military base in Rucano had set free the subversives whom the second lieutenant had captured months before. However, it is now clear to them that those same subversives had been supplying arms to a group of criminals and cattle thieves in Cusco's mountainous region. "And now we urgently need them," says the first captain. "So, we can interrogate them right away," the second captain completes their demand, to make it seem even more peremptory.

The young host, playing dumb, spreads his arms out and confesses that he hasn't the slightest idea what his guests are talking about. "I was half out-of-my-mind when I captured them and now look how I ended up. My head's now almost in the right place, but my body is completely fucked up. Hilario Lara, the older brother of the Francisco you are looking for, tried to break my femur, not too long ago, and because I am a very lucky guy, he only managed to leave me walking with a limp. He's a very dangerous guy." Arrieta explains to the captains, in a very detailed manner, that the people of that region entertain the idea that this Hilario is the devil in the flesh. "Now, I'm out of commission, trying to recuperate, and as such I've lost touch with the reality of which you are speaking to me." The second lieutenant gave two steps to demonstrate that he was barely able to stand on his right foot. "The curious thing is that since I'm no longer worried about these subversives, and have ceased to patrol the border, killing me is no longer a priority for them."

Upon listening to this conversation between the captains and his 'Pops,' Leoncio Quispe, who is sitting on the stone bench attached to the front wall of Arrieta's house, smiles and, introducing himself into the conversation, says to the second lieutenant, that just as he has been telling him repeatedly, no one is really trying to kill them. "You have to believe me, 'Pops,'" he emphasizes, as he articulates the phrase that he uses so often.

The captains ask for some chairs because they say that they have a story to tell. Once the three men are comfortably seated in Gerardo's front yard, the two captains proceed to report to the young officer that the Francisco Lara, of whom they've been speaking, had perished in Ayaviri. This event occurred during a skirmish between the members of an army commando squad and three or four well-armed cattle thieves who had dedicated themselves to rustling cattle from various fiefdoms in that area. The captains expressed in a soft voice, that Francisco Lara exhibited odd behavior, that there was an exchange of gun shots between the soldiers and the "criminals" in the scrubland, close to a small hill called Runa Picchu; that a few minutes after the crossfire commenced, three of the bandits fell dead, shouting: 'Land or Death, until the final victory!'"

The captains explain, before Arrieta's attentive gaze, that Francisco was the only rebel who after that fire-fight was crafty enough to expose himself, with his rifle in hand, in the middle of a clearing in that scrubland. "It was obvious that the person in front of us was out of ammo because he had ceased firing for quite some time, but the man kept insisting on pointing his rifle at us while shouting incessantly, 'land or death!' After the soldiers hesitated for a couple of seconds, all our men, surrounding Lara, felt obligated to shoot him point-blank. There was no alternative. The man pointed his rifle at our commandos with the firm intention of killing them."

Then, they continue: "Our troops left Lara's body full of holes." Both captains then remain silent for the longest three seconds in Arrieta's life. Then, as an afterthought, the first captain says: "The final count was..." To which the second quickly adds, "forty-seven entry wounds," before the first captain can finally conclude their joint-narrative with: "In his entire body." All the while, the alternating voices of his superior officers, effervescing with pride, resonate in Arrieta's ears.

The second lieutenant's interrogators then mention that the moribund Francisco, during his slow descent to the ground beneath his feet, found enough strength to shout: "Gerardo Arrieta, until the final victory" just seconds before he gave up the ghost.

The two captains, scratching their chins to emphasize their cunning, say that they are not sure about the meaning of Francisco's ultimatum. They say that they are unable to figure out if Lara's vociferous last words constitute an obstinate challenge on the part of a dying warrior, or if it was his posthumous homage to a brother-in-arms. They confess that, "to be frank with you, second lieutenant, the motive of this visit of ours is to solve the riddle of Francisco's final pronouncement." The second lieutenant stands up and stares at his superior officers with half-closed eyes. "I have," he says, "real problems to solve. For example," he explains, "I know with certainty the gravity of my situation, because Yatiri, who is the witch-doctor of this fiefdom, has told me that the Devil wants to kill me. My existence has come to revolve around this menace. Therefore, because of my having to defend myself against this demonic threat, do the two of you really believe that I'm going to lose any sleep over what Francisco Lara said upon dying, or over any investigation that you might be able to conduct regarding my possible involvement with the Devil's brother? Do what you want, captains, but while you remain in my garrison I advise you to be very careful once the sun goes down because, in these punas it's truly dangerous to sleep at night. Here we all keep vigil all night long, every day. In this hamlet of Ninantaya, captains, bullets fly and no one ever knows where they came from, or who fired them. The traffic of men and animals in this section of the border is heavy and unpredictable. The cold of the pampa, at night, kills, in a matter of minutes, all those who don't have any friends at hand. I've stumbled over frozen bodies, as stiff as a board, on those nights when it was still possible for me to go on patrol. If I were in your shoes, captains, I'd march out of here immediately, and leave this investigation for a later time."

While the second lieutenant finishes giving his warning to the two captains, Leoncio Quispe (who is still sitting on the stone bench) sighs between smiles, and nods in loyal assent of every word spoken by his friend, the second lieutenant, whom he calls 'Pops.'

VIRGILIO'S FREEDOM

Virgilio knows that he behaved badly. He doesn't wish to imagine what he would do if he had to confront the second lieutenant and account for his activities in the troops' kitchen on that overcast, humid morning. He was trying to put his thoughts together despite the steady patter of hail bouncing off the pebble stone floor of the parade ground. His worry began to grow when a suspicion became nestled in his mind: that Private Quispe had been observing him ever since he came into the kitchen through the back door.

The child is not sure whether Arrieta's orderly had witnessed his actions on that morning; after all, he knows that Quispe is on kitchen patrol every other day. But he prefers to think that if Private Quispe had been there, then the soldier must have entered the kitchen at the precise moment that he was standing in front of the oil burner, dazzled by a raging fire that came out of a greasy nozzle, in the burner's combustion chamber, and traversed the channel under the pots and pans on the stovetop. The boy takes a deep breath and becomes dizzy with the strong smell of fried garlic, rancid grease congealed at the bottom of the empty, unwashed frying pans, and stale water evaporating from the soiled rags with which the cooks clean their serving spoons, ladles, tongs, and spatulas, and dry their hands. What Virgilio fears most is the thought that the soldier might have been spying on him when he extended his right hand, palm facing up and fingers pressed together, holding a reddish-brown feather in the middle of it. Yet, the child relishes the possibility that Arrieta's orderly must have smiled the instant that he blew on this feather, with all the force his lungs could muster, dispatching it into the combustion chamber and the inferno that hid within its sweltering belly.

"But...who knows why Indians laugh?" said the boy to himself. "At times, it is to demonstrate their complicity in the mischievous acts committed by the person they've just observed, while at others it's only because they're scared-to-death of any possible retaliation on the part of the perpetrator. After all, who's going to believe this damn Indian? It's his word against mine, the son of an officer," muttered Virgilio.

* * *

In fact, Quispe had seen everything that the child had done that morning in the troops' kitchen. However, the Private is deeply submerged in a sea of doubt and is unable to come up for air. Virgilio is not the son of just any officer. His father is the major who is second-in-command at Quispe's main operating base in Otabala, while he, just a simple Private on kitchen patrol, is the orderly of Second Lieutenant Arrieta. "Should I tell my 'Pops' about this, or not?"

Quispe doesn't know what to do.... He's afraid. His shred of freedom depends on many people. They could punish him, and he wants to go out on Sunday to see his "cousin"[28] Juanita. "That awful brat," mumbles Private Quispe, "who would have thought? He seemed like a little angel when we first went to Ninantaya. Once there, however, he almost drove the second lieutenant insane," remembers Quispe, shaking his head. "That little shit! I can't control him," the second lieutenant would say every day. "That turd believes that he's entirely independent," Arrieta said bracing his head with both hands, "and he doesn't realize that we all depend on something, on someone."

But the boy just had to do exactly what the second lieutenant had prohibited him from doing ever since they arrived at the hacienda: Do not touch, or even come close to any bird's nest! Because what the Second Lieutenant admired, the most was the freedom enjoyed by wild birds. "If you touch those hatchlings, their mother will kill them, and in many cases, she may even eat them." This is what Second Lieutenant Arrieta told the spoiled child the first day that he arrived at his command post in Ninantaya. It's because the boy's father, Major Rodriguez, had begged the second lieutenant to take the child with him to his forward operating base. He confided to Arrieta that his eight-year-old son drove him crazy by repeating to him every day that the only thing he was in search of was a little freedom. "I'm just looking for a little independence, *papa*" said the major, exemplifying what the little snotnose demanded of him.

Second Lieutenant Arrieta then asked his boss, Major Rodriguez, "And how is it that a snotnose like Virgilio believes that he's going to be free or independent if he travels with me, major?" Rodriguez spoke into Arrieta's ear that the boy doesn't get along very well with his wife. "She doesn't allow him to do anything. She controls his every move," he said in a murmur. "The son-of-a-bitch can't even

---

[28] The indigenous Quechua and Aimara, usually call their girlfriends "prima" (Spanish for female cousin) to hide their real intentions, as if their "patron" saw them as minors who need permission to have a love interest.

breathe on his own without her getting on his case," said the second-in-command, shaking his head with his eyes half-closed and looking down at the ground.

And so, that's how the major obliged the second lieutenant to take the child along with him and whatever needed to happen happened. Virgilio arrived at the troops' quarters on a day when the claps of thunder heard overhead sounded like howitzer blasts, and in the boy's hands was an entire nest with two nestlings huddled in the middle of that straw wreath. They were still naked, without any feathers, much less any down, and at the time Quispe thought that those two little birds would not live to see another day. But, they did. They grew to be fully fledged American kestrels, covered with reddish-brown feathers. The Second Lieutenant cut their wingtips, from time to time, and it's for that reason that they didn't learn to fly. They never flew; that is at least while they remained in the second lieutenant's house.

*   *   *

Virgilio remembers that the second lieutenant became very angry with him and almost blew his top because of the incident involving the nestlings that he brought to the young officer's command post. Arrieta shouted until his face became red and waving his index finger at the level of his temple, he promised the child that he would send him back to his father on the first truck that comes by, without even caring if Virgilio lost his freedom, or not.

"I shit on your freedom, you little turd! You don't deserve to be independent!" Arrieta yelled at him as he threw his field cap onto the ground with uncontrolled rage.

And that's just what Arrieta did, six weeks later. However, until that day arrived Virgilio saw how the Second Lieutenant gradually transformed into the adoptive mother of those raptors. Every morning, in the middle of the damn snowfall that kept them indoors, the young officer would go down to the soldier's quarters and would stuff small bits of sheep's liver into the wide-open beaks of those hatchlings (American kestrel chicks can open their beaks as wide as a door hinge) until their crops looked like ping-pong balls. He fed them in such a painstaking manner that in the blink of an eye they transformed into a couple of big, fat kestrels. The other birds of prey, which were certainly abundant in Ninantaya, would often confuse them with a hen's newly hatched chicks and thus would dive at them to trap those two between their talons.

Virgilio knew that the other birds of prey would never be able to take off with them because even though Arrieta's fledglings couldn't fly they were still able to run like rheas, even on days of intense rain. The Second Lieutenant had trained and spoiled both of those hawks at the same time. It was as if they were truly his sons. He went everywhere with them. These little falcons found refuge upon Arrieta's shoulders, as if they were atop a high, rocky cliff. One could say that they lived there. If someone startled them, they ran like crazy, climbing up his legs and chest before coming back to rest upon his shoulders. If the aggressor approached the second lieutenant, these sparrow hawks would shield themselves behind Arrieta's cranium, later to stick their heads out from behind either of Arrieta's ears and with one eye look at the intruder that threatened them. Virgilio observed every one of the maneuvers of those almost fully-fledged kestrels and muttered between his teeth: "But neither of these dumbasses is able to enjoy any real freedom."

When the young officer at last decided to send Virgilio packing back to MOB Otabala, where his father was, the boy, showing off his resourcefulness, asked the second lieutenant for permission to take one of the critters with him. "Please give me another chance, second lieutenant," he said, already seated in the truck's cab. "I want to show you that I can behave myself...In a humane way, I mean," he almost implored. The second lieutenant contemplated Virgilio with a vacant expression on his face, while he recalled the morning when Private Quispe informed him that he had accidentally discovered that the boy had a horrendous scar on his buttocks, when he saw the kid run, completely naked, from the field shower to his cot in the living room. That same day, while finishing the café latte and bread with cheese that they were having for breakfast, Arrieta asked the boy to stand in the middle of the room, turn around, and drop his pants and underwear to his ankles. "My God!" Arrieta was stunned. He remained speechless and his jaw dropped in that exaggerated way he normally showed his sense of astonishment.

It was there, in the middle of his backside, that the rascal had the mark of a flatiron, stamped in bas-relief. Virgilio gave the two men a very simple explanation: "It's because I'm an ill-mannered boy," he said. "The woman that lives with my father tried to correct me, so that I'll behave better. She let me know that all her actions towards me were well-intentioned. My step-mother tried to explain to me that fire corrects all bad behavior, and upon saying this she thrust the red-hot flatiron right onto my bare ass." Arrieta remained silent for what appeared to be a long period of time, blinking every so often and breathing deeply. It was difficult to say whether he was recalling all the bad things that he'd done in life or he simply could not believe what he was seeing. The young officer had not spoken again of this incident until that day when he bid the boy farewell.

"Poor kid," commented Arrieta to his orderly pointing at Virgilio's rear-end, as the child was walking towards the truck. "I think I now know why this rascal was looking for a bit of freedom," Arrieta remarked to Quispe. "It's got to be hard living with that step-mother," Arrieta said with a sigh. He advanced until he grabbed the vehicle's window with both hands. And he told the boy, very tenderly, to take one of the two raptors off his shoulder. "Take him with you and take good care of him. Don't let his wingtips grow too long or else he'll fly away. It's not that I want to deprive him of his freedom, or his 'independence,' out of any egotistical desire. It's just that these quasi-birds of prey, having been raised in a household, wouldn't know how to coexist with their winged brethren, much less all the other wild critters around them." Then, he told the driver to get out of there, head straight to the house of Major Rodriguez and personally return the child to him, "and make sure to have the major take note that his kid is in one piece and in perfect health."

* * *

Once Second Lieutenant Arrieta had ended his service in the forward operating base of the Ninantaya Hacienda, and returned to his main operating base in Otábala, he found out that Virgilio had lost his sparrow hawk. The child alleged that the bird had been eating more than he should have. "Every single day the soldiers would give him pieces of meat from their lunches and so his wingtips grew back in half the amount of time that they'd normally take to do so," the little scoundrel tried to explain. Virgilio said that it was for those reasons that the bird of prey escaped. "He took off with his winged brethren in search of his freedom, his independence from us," he kept on saying, mimicking the second lieutenant's vocabulary.

Arrieta never knew what happened to either Virgilio's bird, or his own, which also disappeared two days after his return to Otábala. Private Quispe saw his commander suffer so intensely for the loss of his falcon that he felt unable to tell him what he had witnessed in the MOB's kitchen, on a Thursday morning during the worst of a hailstorm. He'd seen Virgilio throwing Arrieta's sparrow hawk into the oil burner's combustion chamber, where the nozzle spits out a flame of at least four hundred degrees, while he said to the little bird in a forceful tone of voice that this was happening because of his bad behavior: "For having wanted to go AWOL in search of freedom, knowing full well that you weren't permitted to do so! Now, you know it! Fire corrects all bad behavior!"

Quispe knew that Virgilio did that. He later saw the boy blowing, from the palm of his hand, a single feather. That feather was all that was left of the kestrel that Second Lieutenant Arrieta had permitted him to bring back from the FOB Ninantaya, and yet never arrived at MOB Otabala, where his father was second in command. According to what the truck driver had told Quispe, the fledgling had escaped when he and Virgilio had stopped to eat at a restaurant in the city of Puno. This happened the same day that he was transporting Virgilio towards the home of his father, Major Rodriguez, at MOB Otabala. The chauffeur also told Arrieta's orderly that along the way, from Ninantaya to Otabala, he had had a long conversation with the kid and that this rascal had told him some very weird things. "He told me that depriving someone of his ability to act according to his free will is not the only way to take away his freedom. You can also do it by robbing him of something very dear to his heart without him having the power to prevent it." The coachman said to Quispe that the funniest thing about it was that during the whole trip

Virgilio kept on repeating: "just wait; in time, the second lieutenant will learn... he'll learn."

BEFORE A WHITE BRICK WALL

The yellow-haired boy enjoys his three years of age. Life at home isn't going at all well, but even so, he is still unaware that simple day-to-day occurrences are often capable of destroying one's happiness in what it takes a rooster to crow. Up to this point, his biggest complaint had arisen one day when his dearest aunt, Gertrudis, asked him to drink his midafternoon café latte from a baby bottle under the scrutiny of three other women who were playing canasta with her in the living room. The boy's aunt asked him, three times in a row, but each time that he emphatically answered "no," she refused to acknowledge him. And so, after his aunt insisted a fourth time, manifesting her authority as the lady of the house, the child took hold of the glass baby bottle and smashed it on the hardwood floor.

Since the boy is an only child (on top of the fact that he is also the only nephew that his several, full-grown aunts have) and he doesn't have any cousins or friends who are his age, his vocabulary and personality appear to mimic those of the adults around him. Sometimes, he acts in such an aggressive manner that he surprises any visitors who come to the house. For example, when he says "no," in response to something that he's been asked to do, he in fact believes that people should understand that "no" means "no."

The aunt's friends comment: "What a vocabulary he has, my dear Gertrudis!" "Where does this snotnose get such big words that even I find difficult to pronounce?" And the aunt explains that the child stays close to her and her sisters most of the time. "Y'all know that all of us have always enjoyed speaking with a proper and fine Castilian Spanish." And then comes in her younger sister with the corroborating evidence: "When I read the novels I like, I do it aloud, and this little turd[29] sits next to me and not only listens, but also asks me questions. He makes me repeat, several times, whatever passages spark his curiosity."

There are days when the child cries for no apparent reason. His wailing is continuous, insistent, and monotonous. At these times, his mother rushes diligently to his side to lavish her attention upon him. She speaks to the boy in a sweet tone of voice and caresses him, but to no avail. "You just have to let him pour his little heart out," she says to herself, alleging that the child, with his stubborn moaning, gives her an infernal migraine that's impossible for her to mitigate. "There has to be correlation between my headache and his obstinate crying," she says when she shuts herself up in her bedroom.

* * *

His father travels often. The man is a truck driver. When he's at home, for one or two weeks every four months, the kid's sense of peace and quiet in his household temporarily evaporates. During these moments when the family is once again complete, the yellow-haired boy becomes resentful. It's because his father treats him poorly, yells at him, and on some occasions even gives him a

---

[29] In the city of Arequipa, the locals use the word 'turd', as a term of endearment, when speaking with, or about, small children.

spanking on the rear-end. And when he resorts to corporal punishment, he does so, according to the child, "with an extraordinary show of force." However, what the kid finds to be most offensive of all is that when his father visits them, the little fellow finds himself obligated to sleep alone, in a hard, narrow bunk that is assembled for him next to his parents' conjugal bed. Because of this "unjust and arbitrary" decision, as this boy calls it, he is unable to sleep alongside his mother.

The aunts surrounding his mother shield him from any accusations, and acquiesce to all his whims. For example, his Christmases are unbelievable. He receives so many gifts that he's unable to count them all. The most difficult part of these gatherings comes after the festivities have ended and he must carry all his presents from the house of his aunts back to his own home. The child drags, over the course of several trips, a weathered burlap sack into which he keeps putting all the toys that the child Jesus[30] brought him the night before.

*　*　*

The house of the yellow-haired child is long, old, and dirty. The dwelling consists of a succession of rooms, the last of which are mere spaces crammed, from floor-to-ceiling, with: old, urine stained mattresses; crippled chairs; broken-down, greasy stoves; couches full of holes showing protruding coiled springs; bicycles with no wheels; a disassembled engine from a 1932 Ford pickup truck; piles of dirty, old T-shirts; bundles of sheep's wool; malodorous and unusable blankets; and several families of rats. It is among those heaps of rags and broken furniture that the boy

---

[30] In Latin America, in the 1940's, before Santa Claus was imported from the United States, it was thought that it was the child Jesus who brought everyone presents on the night of Christmas Eve.

usually plays hide-and-seek with the prepubescent maidservant.

Yet, his favorite place is found in the backyard, at the foot of the cherry tree, next to a white brick wall. Every morning, the child goes out to gather any ripe cherries that fell the night before. "I would like to live forever in this place," the child says. Afterwards, he sits under the shade produced by the abundant cherry leaves matted above his head and entertains himself by organizing snail races.

This coming Christmas Eve promises to be much better than the previous one. His parents have replaced the Aimara maidservant that they had (they say that the girl was too much of a crybaby) with an Aimara youngster who came from the town of Rucano, near Lake Titicaca, and who answers to the name of Hilario. This teenager had promised the yellow-haired child that at the end of the year he would do him the favor of carrying all the toys (which he had heard that the boy usually collects from his aunts) back to his parents' house, and even all the way to his bedroom. "Something tells me that this is going to be the beginning of a beautiful relationship," said the new servant with a devious half-smile.

* * *

The last time that his father came to the house, the young one witnessed an event that both frightened him and left him perplexed. He was fully awake, at midnight, drenched in sweat and agitated because he had just come out of a terrible nightmare, when he heard his father asking his mother (insistently and in a low tone of voice) to take off her panties. Each time that he asked her, she resolutely rejected his demands. His father persisted in his requests until he got what he wanted. The child listened, motionless,

161

in absolute silence, while he asked himself why his father made such a nonsensical demand as to ask someone to take off her underpants. Driven by the desire to avoid being reprimanded by his father's stentorian voice, the child held his breath and remained immobile.

The darkness of the room was of such a degree that the only thing he could see was the contours of the bodies before him, like hills on the horizon at the darkest hour of the night. Soon, the kid became a witness to the spasmodic and frenetic movements of the protuberances that he could distinguish on the bed that was right next to his. Also, he heard how his father promised his mother to make her an additional son. Then, there arose, within the boy's infantile brain, a question that had never occurred to him before: "How are children made?" he thought as he silently moved his lips.

*   *   *

Hilario tries, by any means available to him, to spend as much of his time playing with the yellow-haired child. That's why the kid doesn't cry as much, and yet his mother's sisters fear that something bad could come about from the proximity of this disparate pair. "These filthy *cholos* all have very bad customs," his aunts tend to say between sips of tea.

Old Liberata, the aunts' Aimara maidservant, comments with her toothless mouth, as she slowly drags her right foot behind her, that small children can learn incurable habits when they can spend so much time with adults who are unfamiliar with one's household customs. It's because, she says, as she wags her right index finger, "these adults themselves are practically unfamiliar to us." Then she continues saying that: "This pair spends almost the whole day together. Nothing good can come of it. This relationship, as innocent as it may seem, could destroy us all."

* * *

There is something that's disturbing the yellow-haired child. Every time his father stays at home between trips, he can't sleep next to his mother. Sleeping alone, during these intervals in time, is terrifying for him, because when he does so the child suffers the most horrible of nightmares. In these dreams, the Devil comes for him with a red-hot iron trident, and hunts him down inexorably. The child tosses and turns between his sheets, trying to free himself from the talons of that monstrous vision.

* * *

The boy began to lose his loquacious nature after the third month of playing with Hilario, the new servant. His mother and aunts ask him what happened to the boy they used to know who was so talkative and happy, but the child avoids looking at them face to face and only says that he has nothing to talk about. Yet, deep down, and secretly, he has a lot to fear. In those last few weeks, his friend Hilario pesters him with a proposition. The lad doesn't know what to do. Before Hilario came into his life, the young boy's loneliness had been such that he fears returning to that miserable state. By that moment, he had already come to know what it's like to have a playmate for an entire day. The anguish that impedes him from being more communicative is rooted in the complexity of the decision that he must make. If he acquiesces to Hilario's proposition,

163

he would be able to live in an eternity of fun and games. On the other hand, if he doesn't, Hilario threatens never to play with him again. "If you don't comply with what I'm asking you to do, then I'll tell you that I was only hired to cook and run errands, and not to play with and entertain any little brat," he says with a wrinkled brow and the boy begins to have doubts.

*   *   *

The yellow-haired kid doesn't quite understand some of the words that his 'friend' Hilario is using. However, he intuits that there are certain things which the young man is proposing him to do that appear to have, from a logical standpoint (as his aunts would say), a malicious undertone. But, despite his doubts and his increasing curiosity, he prefers not to bring this matter to either his aunts' or his mother's attention. "I could be severely beaten by them," he mutters between his teeth as he chews the nail on his ring finger.

*   *   *

Hilario doesn't give up. He keeps on insisting and invites the infant to play with him; he proposes an activity that will allow them both to mimic the movies they see on Sundays, before noon. "You're going to be Captain Marvel," he says, and the kid's face lights up, as he sticks his chest out and strikes it with his little fists, shouting with excitement: "I'm the Shazam guy!"

After a while, once the two 'friends' are totally immersed in their theatrical reinterpretation, the Aimara servant suggests to the child that he can teach him how to fly like his cinematic hero. He takes the boy into his arms, with one hand under his chest while the other holds up the child's thighs, as he promises him that he'll fulfill his fantasy of flying. As Hilario walks carrying his human airplane towards the backyard, the child observes the hardwood floor; the loose dirt that surrounds the cherry tree; his mother's flowerpots; and then he imagines that he sees mountain chains, valleys, and rivers; he finds himself filled with the sensation that he is floating among the clouds, and he enjoys the view of planet Earth, underneath.

*　*　*

The aunts, who little by little were beginning to accept Hilario, enthusiastically comment about the love that the young servant has for the yellow-haired child. "What dedication!" one of his aunts exclaims. "He spends all of his free time with the child after doing his chores around the house." With a smile, Hilario solicits the admiration of the adults in the household, while also gaining the full trust of the child. "They have an impeccable friendship," say the aunts with a look of utmost satisfaction on their faces.

*　*　*

Suddenly, Hilario doesn't want to play anymore. He says that he is tired, that he has other things to do, and that he'll play again another day. Saddened by this, the child asks and begs Hilario to spend time with him without receiving any answer that can make him understand what he's done to displease the young servant in such a horrible way. Nonetheless, the boy keeps on demanding that the two of them play together like they used to do, until the yellow-haired kid eventually decides that he should try to placate the servant by conceding to *his* initial propositions: "What is it that you want me to do, Hilario, so that you'll play with me?" asks the boy, on the verge of tears.

Hilario stands upright and laconically states: "You have to jerk off." The kid remains silent. He looks at the floor and recalls the many times that Hilario has asked him to do that same thing, below the dining table, at supper time. Being but a mere four years old, the child is unable to find any sense or justification whatsoever for rubbing his weenie. Moreover, he thinks that if that's what it takes Hilario to play with him, "I'll have to do it then," he mutters between his teeth as he undoes his suspenders to drop his high-cuffed shorts.

* * *

Two weeks have passed and the child is very worried because Hilario doesn't want to comply with the deal that they made days before. "Some sort of milk has to come out of your weenie," the servant shouts, and the boy shrinks back in fear. "You have to do it really hard until that milky stuff comes out. That's when we'll know if you're a real man and, at the same time, you'll see how great it feels." Hilario whispers into the boy's ear with a mellifluous voice. "Or perhaps you are a woman; which is not bad in and of itself...but if you are in fact a woman, I'll have to put a child inside your belly, so that you'll learn how babies are made," threatens Hilario, as he lets out a guffaw. The little one feels guilty. He doesn't understand what Hilario's requiring him to do and every day that passes he feels increasingly fearful, and ashamed to speak with his mother, or his aunts, so that they'll defend him, so that they'll save him, so that they'll replace the *cholo* who cleans their house.

Hilario tells the yellow-haired child that he's tired of waiting. That he's going to tell his mother and all his aunts what he does every afternoon with his weenie. Terror fills the boy's heart and he wants to cry. Hilario observes him and accelerates the pace of his discourse. "I'm going to tell them all right now," he says and begins to walk toward the house. The child cries out with a heart-breaking expression on his face, and says, no. "Please, no," he implores the servant, between sobs. And so, Hilario switches out the malevolent expression on his face for one of even-tempered compassion. He approaches the boy, takes him into his arms and murmurs words of love, as he makes his way towards his assigned bedroom and the child, finding himself so tenderly caressed, begins to calm down. "Not to your bedroom!" complains the little boy, sensing himself to be a prey to his own fear: "My mother already told me that I should never go there!" he says in a low voice, squirming like a serpent. But Hilario continues to imprison him with his arms; he opens the door of his quarters and enters with the child.

Having crossed the threshold of his bedroom, Hilario tells the child that his clothes are soaked from all the little tears that he's wept. "We're going to have to change your clothes so that nobody finds out that you've been crying," says the servant, beginning to undress the boy with the formality of a religious ceremony. Once he has the child completely naked, Hilario begins to caress him all over. Then, he kisses his belly, his buttocks, and lastly, he sucks his weenie.

The yellow-haired boy, paralyzed with fear, doesn't know what to do. He feels as if his mind is immersed in a vat of tar that prevents him from thinking swiftly. He doesn't know which way to turn. He finds himself caught in between the need to earn the kindness of the person that holds him with such tenacity, and his fear of what will happen next. When Hilario begins to loosen his belt, the boy sees that the Indian has the face of Satan and he foresees his future. The infant unfreezes himself from the paralysis that had petrified him, upon discovering in the deepest recesses of his mind that Hilario, or the Devil (he's not able to tell which) wants to turn him into a woman.

And so, he takes off running and leaves the bedroom, desperate. As he is naked, he doesn't look for his mother or aunts. The shame that he would he feel would be too great. He turns left towards the garden. He thinks about the cherry tree that stands next to the white brick wall. "I will climb up to the very top," he says, "and the *cholo* won't be able to get me." But Hilario, who's running with a longer pair of legs than the child, catches up with him and envelopes the yellow-haired boy in his arms. They both hit the ground and wrestle on the soft earth of the untended garden. The young Aimara servant, with all the energy of his sixteen years of age, takes hold of the child from behind and possesses him by force. The child lets out a scream of pain as his blood flows and spreads all over his aggressor's pants. Hilario, with the boy firmly in his grip, turns his head in desperation, in search of the child's mother and the aunts, and continues to revel in his sexual feast.

To impede the child's screams, the servant submerges his little head into the dead earth that is as loose as talcum powder. The small boy stopped yelling. He coughs, chokes, convulses, and finally his body stiffens as his life appears to reach its end at the very moment in which Hilario enjoys an orgasm that he had been striving to obtain since he first arrived at that house.

* * *

The young assailant senses a series of shouts approaching him. He zips up the fly of his pants, cleans the blood off his hands, and covers the body of the yellow-haired boy with dry leaves and twigs. He stands up and runs out of the garden as fast as he can. In the entrance hall, before reaching the door facing the street, he comes across the oldest of the child's aunts, armed with a broom stick. He continues his wild escape, but the blood stains on his clothes give him away. The aunt asks about the child. She cries out, wails, weeps, and charges towards Hilario, beating him with her innocent weapon.

* * *

Hilario was arrested by a gendarme at the door of the house, just a second before he reached the street. The judge sentenced him to a term of nine years in prison, adding that it could later be reduced to a four-year term depending on his good behavior. The magistrate explained that the sentence was light, given that the accused was a minor, and as such, he, as a judge, considered that at sixteen years of age, Hilario was still incapable of discerning between good and evil.

The yellow-haired child's oldest aunt, the one who confronted Hilario when he was trying to escape, relates that when she charged at the Indian servant she looked him in the eyes and was certain that they were as red and luminous as two glowing embers. She also says that when the *cholo* ran past her, the smell was unbearable. It was as if the youngster had just come back from working in the vineyards of her father, Don Gerardo, where he was spreading sulfur over the vines to keep the fungi from causing them as much damage as they usually tend to do.

* * *

Over the years, the details, and contents of the story about what had happened that day, slowly mutated in much the same way in which myths are constructed by all small communities throughout history. No one knows for sure whether the child (named at birth, Gerardito, like his Grandfather) died, or not. Some say that he did, and that he was buried in a beautiful, white coffin; that the aunts mourned for years the death of their beloved nephew, and that the mother, unable to overcome her grief, found herself submerged in a state of madness. On the other hand, there are those that say that the yellow-haired boy was saved; that his mama Gertrudis, the sister of his actual mother, brought him back to life by blowing air into his lungs, through his mouth, for hours, until in one of those attempts to resuscitate him, the child awoke, stood up, walked a bit, and said: "I'm hungry, give me something to eat." However, the boy never remembered what had happened to him. It was as if another soul, that by chanced was passing by, had entered that still-warm little body while the original spirit, that of the yellow-haired child, took off believing that it was no longer possible for it to live in that abused body; a body, which according to the outgoing spirit was now that of a woman, and as such had ceased to be the dwelling where it had resided as a happy child, for a little over four years.

ABOUT THE AUTHOR

Manuel Aguirre (Arequipa, 1940), is a retired officer of the Peruvian Army since 1972.

Between the years 1971 and 1976, he traveled to, and lived in, France, Hungary, and Spain. In 1978, he earned a master's degree in business administration at ESAN, in Lima, Peru. While in that city he worked in banks and insurance companies until 1987. In August of that year, he emigrated to the U.S., where he lived in California until May 2013. He currently resides in Oxford, MS with his wife and youngest son.

In 1972, he published in Lima, Peru, a book of poems titled *Razón de silencio* (Author's Edition). In 2006, Manuel Aguirre published in Lima, Peru, his first novel *Una bala en la frente*, with the publishing house Estruendo Mudo. In 2007, he published *Reyertas y desafíos*, a book of short stories, with the publishing house El Santo Oficio. In 2010, the publishing house Les Fondeurs de Briques translated *Una bala en la frente* into French (as, *Une balle dans le front*) and published it in France where it received an excellent literary review from the famous literary critic, Mathieu Lindon, in the pages of the nationally syndicated newspaper *Liberation* (October 21[st,] 2010).

In April 2013, the publishing house Planeta-Perú published, in Spanish, a revised and augmented version of *Una bala en la frente*, in Lima, Peru. In 2016, Manuel Aguirre published, in Lima, Peru, a second novel, *Insurgente* (Author's Edition), which is the second novel of his Saga, *Dudas y murmuraciones (Doubts and Murmurs)*. He is currently working on the third novel of that Saga, which will be titled *Crisol.*

THE SAGA

Doubts and Murmurs (Dudas y murmuraciones) is a Saga (that consists of three novels) which examines life in the Peruvian Army in three of its various possible stages.

1. *A Bullet in His Forehead* (*Una bala en la* frente): Service in a Forward Operating Base. An officer and ten soldiers with the objective of observing, reporting on, and at the same time safeguarding the integrity of the nation's border.

2. *Insurgent* (*Insurgente*): Service on a military installation, or Main Operating Base, in which said officer shares in his functions as such with a good number of colleagues, commanders, and enlisted troops.

3. Crisol (*Crucible*): Enrollment at a Service Academy during four to five years at the end of which one will obtain the rank of second lieutenant.

www.ingramcontent.com/pod-product-compliance
Lightning Source LLC
Chambersburg PA
CBHW030258130626
46549CB00002B/595